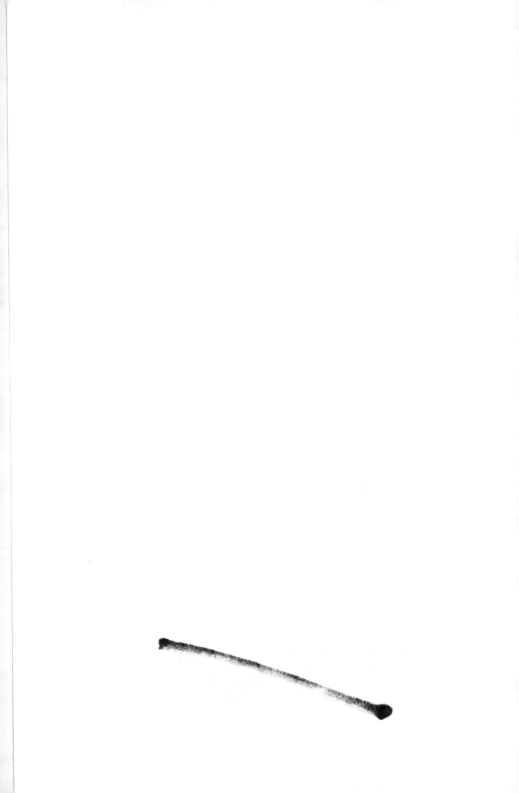

IN THE VALLEY OF
THE KINGS

[*stories*]

TERRENCE HOLT

W. W. NORTON & COMPANY

New York · London

For information about permission to reproduce selections from this book,
write to Permissions, W. W. Norton & Company, Inc.,
500 Fifth Avenue, New York, NY 10110

For information about special discounts for bulk purchases, please contact
W. W. Norton Special Sales at specialsales@wwnorton.com or 800-233-4830

Manufacturing by Courier Westford
Book design by Chris Welch
Production manager: Anna Oler

Library of Congress Cataloging-in-Publication Data

Holt, Terrence.
In the Valley of the Kings : stories / Terrence Holt. — 1st ed.
p. cm.
ISBN 978-0-393-07121-4
I. Title.
PS3608.O4943598I52 2009
813'.6—dc22
2009023461

W. W. Norton & Company, Inc.
500 Fifth Avenue, New York, N.Y. 10110
www.wwnorton.com

W. W. Norton & Company Ltd.
Castle House, 75/76 Wells Street, London W1T 3QT

1 2 3 4 5 6 7 8 9 0

FOR LAURIE

CONTENTS

ACKNOWLEDGMENTS

Hippocrates reminds us to remember our teachers with gratitude, and I gladly thank them first. Mark Dintenfass, Alison Lurie, James McConkey, Dan McCall, Walter Slatoff, and Harold Brodkey all have a hand in whatever virtues these stories possess. Ellen Schwamm gave invaluable assistance when I was learning to edit; "Charybdis" would never have gotten off the ground without her aid.

The individuals and agencies who have provided material assistance include: the Djerassi Foundation, and Carl Djerassi in particular; the Fine Arts Work Center at Provincetown; the Pennsylvania State Council for the Arts; and finally, to Grace Paley, for her customary generosity, encouragement, and support: thank you.

Ron Sharp and Frederick Turner of *The Kenyon Review*, William Abrahams of Doubleday's O. *Henry Prize Stories* series, Stanley Lindberg and Stephen Corey of *The Georgia Review*, Mary Kinzie and Reginald Gibbons of *TriQuarterly*, and Adrienne Brodeur and Samantha Schnee of *Zoetrope* all helped shape these pieces and sustain my career.

Robert Weil at Norton has been the *beau ideal* of an editor. His insight into these stories has been invaluable.

It is impossible to thank Nicole Aragi adequately. I can only say that it is through her that I have come to understand the doctrine of grace.

And to Junot Díaz, for rewarding my stumbling efforts on his behalf far more than they deserved: thank you, even though you persist in calling me "Professor."

Constance Holt knows far better than I how much she helped this book into being, but let this serve as a reminder to both of us.

Toby and Theo entered these stories at different points in their development, and added new reasons for finishing them. Thank you for keeping me awake so much of the time.

Laurie's contribution to these stories is difficult to explain. That's why I wrote them. And why I needed her to make sense of them. Thank you.

Ὁ Λόγος

Videtur quod Author hic obiit.

The first case of which any record survives was reported in a small-town daily in upstate New York. Tabitha Van Order, the brief item reads, age five, was brought into the county hospital's emergency room with "strange markings" on her face and hands. "She was playing with the newspaper," her mother reported. "I thought it was just the ink rubbed off on her." But the marks did not respond to soap or turpentine. At the hospital, initial examination determined that the marks were subcutaneous, and the child was admitted for observation. They looked, according to the triage nurse, as though someone had been striking the child with a large rubber stamp. "They look like bruises," the emergency-room physician told the *Journal* reporter. The department of social services was looking into the case.

This alone might not have warranted even three inches on page eight of a sixteen-page paper. What attracted the attention of the editor at the county desk (whose sister, a nurse in the E.R., had phoned in the story), and earned Tabitha's case even that scanty initial notice, was one peculiar feature of those bruises, one fact about the case that stood out from the face of an otherwise unremarkable, seemingly healthy little girl. It was not that, over the next several days, the marks did not fade, nor exhibit any of the changes of hue or outline usual in a bruise—although this was puzzling. Nor was it the child's silence, which she maintained three days with a patient gravity that impressed the most casual of observers. What claimed the attention of everyone who saw the child over the three days of her illness was the unmistakable pattern in those marks. They formed a word.

A word, certainly: no one who saw doubted for an instant what they saw. And it was something more, as well. Everyone struck with the sight of that pale, silent face and that black sign reported the same response: each said that the shock of seeing it for the first time was almost physical. It was as if, the nurse on the day shift recalled, seeing it, you felt it on your own face— "like a blush." And indeed, after the initial shock, something like embarrassment did set in: the nurses could never bring themselves to utter the word, either to the child or among themselves; the physicians during their morning rounds half averted their eyes even as they palpated the affected areas. And although *bruises* were discussed day and night across the desk at the nursing station; although *palpable purpura* were the subject of long discussions in the cafeteria; although everyone down to the orderlies hazarded a guess as to the nature of the marks, the word itself went euphemized, persistently elided.

After embarrassment there followed another response, something of which communicates itself even now in the tone of that first newspaper article, a kind of delicacy, a reticence over the details of the case: a hush. That respectful silence grows ambivalently louder in the two pieces that in as many days followed, lengthened, and moved forward toward page one. As for the child herself, she made no complaint, nor in fact did she utter any word at all until just before the end, when she was heard to pronounce, in tones audible as far as the nursing station, the word spelled out by the bruise across her hands, cheeks, jaw, and (most plainly) forehead. She spoke the word in a piercing falsetto three times, and then, before the nurse could reach the room, the child coded, as the physician's assistant said, and died.

I LEARNED MUCH of this, of course, later, by which time several of the principals—the nurses, the orderlies, the mother, and the physicians—were beyond the reach of my own inquiries. But I believe the editor told me as much of the truth as he knew before he died.

Which was more than he told his readers. Even in the third article, which appeared on the fourth day following Tabitha's admission to the hospital, and where the headline type has grown to fifty-four points, the text is most significant for what it does not say. It does not tell the precise form of those bruises that darkened across the child's features in her last twelve hours and then faded completely within minutes of her death—although the darkening and the fading both are faithfully set down. Nor does it transcribe the syllables the child voiced three times before she died—although the fact of her crying out is also given. It does not even mention that the bruises formed a word.

There was this aspect of the affair notable from the start: the embarrassment that overcame all who saw the word, as if the thing were shameful. Not, I believe, for what it said, but for being so patently, inscrutably significant: for being a sign. Few people could bring themselves, at first, even to acknowledge what they saw. It was as if an angel had planted one bare foot in Central Park, another on the Battery, and cast the shadow of a brazen horn over Newark. If such had happened, how many minutes might we suppose to have elapsed before anyone could have brought himself to turn to his neighbor and ask, —Do you see?—How could any of us discuss it without feeling implicated? So it was in the case of Tabitha's word: it was too plainly part of a world we no longer knew how to address.

But there was more to this evasion, of course, than met the eye, and it is this that I find truly remarkable about the case. It is the function of that evasion, and the unmistakable conclusion it urges, that most impresses me: that everyone who saw the word, immediately, without understanding, without conscious thought or any evidence at all, knew that to see the word in print was a sentence of death.

No one, at the time, had any empirical reason for suspecting such, but in every account, even the first, I trace an instinctive recognition that it was the word itself that carried the contagion. It was several months, of course, before the means of transmission was identified, through the work of the Centers for Disease Control and Prevention in Atlanta and Lucerne, and ultimately the heroic sacrifice of the interdisciplinary team at the *École des Hautes Études en Sciènces Sociales* in Paris. So how do we find, in this first written record, the prudence that spared until a later date so many lives? And how do we balance that seeming prudence with the other inescapable fact about the word: that as the end approached, all seemed seized—as was Tabitha herself—with an impulse to speak. It was as if the word struggled to speak itself, as if in answer to some drive to propagate that would not be denied.

The elucidation of the mechanism was complicated by the discovery that mere speech was harmless, as was hearing: it was the eye through which the plague entered, and the eye alone. The hand that wrote, so long as the person behind it did not look, was spared (with the notorious exception of the blind, who took the illness in Braille, and broke out before they died in portentous boils). But to see the word in print (ink or video, it did not matter) was to sicken, and invariably to die.

Experimental studies were hampered, of course, by a number of complicating factors, not least of which was the obvious difficulty in conducting tests on other than human subjects. A late attempt was made, by some accounts, to incorporate the word into the ideogrammatic code taught to chimpanzees at the Yerkes National Primate Center; results were fragmentary, the experiment ending prematurely with the incapacitation of the staff. One significant datum did emerge from all studies, however: illiteracy was no defense. Even those incapable of deciphering the dialogue from comic strips were found to be susceptible. The only exceptions were those functioning, for whatever reason, below the mental age of thirty months.

But all of this knowledge came later. Although this most important aspect of the disease did ultimately receive full measure of publicity, in the case of Tabitha Van Order the initial reports were mute. Indeed, were it not owing to the early curiosity of one researcher in virology at a nearby university, the epidemiological particulars of this first case might have passed almost entirely unrecorded. This virologist, one Taylor Salomon, happened to have been a patient on the same floor as the child, incapacitated with a pneumonia contracted while at work in her laboratory. On the day that Tabitha gave up the ghost in a room four doors down from hers, Professor Salomon was sitting up in bed for the first time in two weeks, taking some clear broth and attempting to organize notes from her research.

The attempt was futile, owing to the extreme weakness that had kept her semiconscious for the previous two weeks, and was disrupted forever by the unearthly cry that heralded Tabitha's demise. Professor Salomon was fortunate in this, however: her own illness had kept her from visiting the child's room, or even glimpsing her mottled face through the open door before the marks had faded entirely away. And the research project that had hospitalized Professor Salomon soon faded from her thoughts as well, supplanted by a new question as soon as the nurse appeared, visibly shaken, in answer to the professor's call.

The nurse could report the sequel of the child's cry, but

not its meaning; she could only echo, with the distracted air that had come to typify the medical staff in the last hours of Tabitha's life, the helpless distress of her colleagues at finding their patient so unaccountably dead. To Salomon's more pertinent questions about the disease's course and etiology, the nurse could only wring her hands and look back over her shoulder, as if she harbored a guilty secret. Her curiosity piqued, Dr. Salomon managed to rise from her bed and stumble down the hall before the orderlies arrived to wheel the body away. The marks had apparently disappeared no more than five minutes before her arrival.

Luck was with her again, in that her appearance in the room was followed almost immediately by that of the medical examiner. The examiner, already irritated at the interruption of lunch, was inclined to order Salomon from the room, and her recitation of her credentials did nothing, at first, to soothe him. But being in no mood to take up the investigation himself, even in his irritation he was no match for Salomon's persistence, and in the end he agreed to provide the samples she required. In an additional example of the good fortune that marked so much of Salomon's involvement with the case, the M.E.'s cooperative attitude was not shared by the hospital staff, which refused to release the child's chart to anyone but the M.E., citing doctor-patient confidentiality. But the samples, Salomon felt, would prove more valuable than any M.D.'s scribble, and she was content with the oral recitation of the child's history she eventually wrung from the nurses. The samples, iced and isolated according to protocols, waited another two weeks before Salomon was able to return to her lab, where she found, of course, nothing. The blood, nerve tissue, and other fragments of Tabitha's clay were apparently those of a healthy five-year-old girl, and nothing an extremely well-funded laboratory could bring to bear on them was able to add anything to the story.

Stymied in the laboratory, Salomon turned to a colleague in epidemiology, and, swearing him to secrecy, initiated field studies of the child's home, school, and other haunts. The season was late spring; the child's back yard abutted on a swamp: insect traps were set and their prey examined (at this point the impromptu task force expanded to include an entomologist). Once again, nothing significant appeared.

Time was running out for Salomon and her hope of scoring a coup. Five weeks after Tabitha's admission to the hospital, the child's mother, the triage nurse, four orderlies, the emergency-room physician's assistant, three floor nurses and two doctors were admitted with livid bruises on the palms of their hands, cheeks, jaws, and (most plainly) foreheads.

In this first wave of cases, the disease exhibited additional symptoms, not observed (or not reported) in the case of Tabitha Van Order. In the triage nurse, onset was marked by a vague dreaminess that overtook her at work one morning. By lunchtime, she was incapable of entering insurance information correctly on her forms, and by midafternoon she had wandered from her desk. She was found on one of the high floors of the hospital, staring out a window at the lake, where a sailboat regatta was in progress. It was only at this point that the marks on her face were noticed. At about this time (the precise time is unavailable, owing to the nurse's absence from her desk),

Julia Van Order arrived at the emergency room, brought in by a neighbor who had found her laughing uncontrollably in the street outside her home. The third symptom, glossolalia, was observed in two of the orderlies and one physician, who were admitted over the course of the evening. By midnight, there were twelve patients on the floor.

Recognizing an incipient epidemic, the chief of infectious disease imposed strict quarantine that evening. Staff on the floor were issued the customary isolation gear, and strict contact precautions were imposed. Who could blame the man for not issuing blindfolds? Such measures were in fact tried, much later, but by then, of course, it was much too late. He failed as well to confiscate pens.

Professor Salomon, on hearing of these new admissions, realized that her time was running out, and did the only thing left to her. After one visit to the hospital, during which she conducted interviews with those of the victims able to respond, she wrote up as full a description of the disease as she could, took her best guess (which turned out, in the end, to be wrong) as to its cause, sealed the four closely-printed pages in a dated envelope, and sent it, with a cover letter, to the *New England Journal of Medicine*. It was not at that time the policy of the *New England Journal* to accept so-called *plis cachetés*, the practice having fallen into disrepute over a generation earlier, and Salomon's contribution might have been returned unopened had it not been for yet another fortuitous circumstance.

A reporter specializing in science and medicine for a national news magazine was visiting Salomon's university that week, lecturing graduate students in journalism. On the day he was scheduled to return to New York, he happened to hear of the dozen deaths that had occurred the previous night at the county hospital. Sensing a career opportunity, he filed a story, complete with an interview with Salomon, and the item ran prominently in the *Health* section of the following week's issue.

The reporter, who had conducted his interviews with the hospital staff over the phone, and filed in the same way, was fortunate. Professor Salomon was not; time had in fact run out for her in more ways than one. Before she died, however, she had the satisfaction of seeing her report in print, its publication in the *New England Journal* spurred on by the article in *Time*.

In the four weeks that followed the first wave, mortality in the county was misleadingly low. The local daily never having printed the word, the contagion was spread almost exclusively among the hospital staff, in whom the disease lay latent for the month of July. At the end of the first week of August, the marks broke out over the hands, cheeks, jaws, and (most prominently) foreheads of approximately eighty-five doctors, nurses, orderlies, speech therapists and social workers, most of whom were brought in by their families in various stages of confusion, euphoria, and glossolalia.

In this second wave, observers reported yet another symptom, which followed those exhibited in the first wave in a distinct progression. Whether the onset was marked by dreamy confusion, giddiness, or fluently unintelligible speech, within twelve hours all such symptoms had lapsed into one: an uncontrollable paranoia, in which the sufferer was convinced that every object in the world, animate or inanimate, was involved in a vast conspiracy to do the patient harm.

Without exception, in this stage of the disease its victims spoke continuously for periods of up to twenty-four hours, offering elaborately detailed descriptions of the delusional system in which they were enmeshed. And without exception, the attending physicians reported that they had at times to fight off the conviction that their patients' nightmares were real. Who can blame them? Confronted with an undeniable health emergency, swift to spread, invariably fatal, and marked at its heart by the inscrutable symbol of the word, little wonder that those who struggled to understand the disease struggled as well with fear. Unlike their patients, who had evolved an explanation for the menace within them, their doctors had no such comfort, and could only watch their patients die, and wonder helplessly if they had contracted the plague as well.

For plague, by the end of the first week of September, it had become. There is little point in going over the statistics of that hellish week: the figures beggar comprehension, and mere repetition will not suffice to make them meaningful. Certainly their import was dulled by the more immediate, personal tragedies that struck almost every household in the country at that time. And as the numbers grew to embrace other nations, other languages, their meaning became in no way more intelligible. No more than did the word, which, as it appeared in different nations, took on different forms, but had everywhere the same effect.

AT THIS TIME, little remains to report, but I would like to offer before I close two or three items that strike me as significant. The first, as I have hinted, was almost lost in the events that followed so quickly on the disease's emergence into the public eye. But Professor Salomon's team, in the weeks between her death and theirs, continued its research into the origins of the contagion. And though the trail had by then grown cold, the scent was not so faint that they could find in this an excuse for the failure of their investigations: the disease was untraceable, they concluded, because it had no physical cause.

And here I find one of the most pathetic effects of this disease—the kind of case in which its action was so grievous because so clearly marked. One of Salomon's survivors, a geneticist, whom I had known slightly during our years together at the university, and who was one of the few men I have ever met who might have deserved to be called a genius, telephoned me on the day the disease took hold of him. While I kept him on the phone, in the thirty minutes before help arrived I listened as he spun out the delusion that had come on him with the word. The spectacle, if I may call it that, of a mind of his caliber reduced to raving brought me close to tears.

But I feel obligated to report what he said to me that day, in part because it was my only immediate contact with a victim of the plague. And also because one aspect of the encounter still strikes me, somehow, as significant. I believed. All the time I was speaking to him, I found myself fighting off conviction. Naturally, the feeling passed, but I still find myself, several weeks later, struggling with a sense of opportunity missed: I felt at the time, and still in my weaker moments do, as though I had come close to penetrating the mystery of the word. This is, of course, one of the effects most frequently reported by those attending on the dying.

The disease, my caller insisted, was not, properly speaking, a plague. That is to say, it was not spread by any of the infectious mechanisms. The word was not a pathogen: it was a catalyst, and the disease itself immanent in humanity at large. He had deciphered a sequence, he claimed, in the human genome, which matched, in the repetitive arrangement of its amino acids, the structure of the word. It seemed the word, processed in the temporal lobe in the presence of sufficient quantities of norepinephrine—the quantities released at levels of anxiety commonly associated with imminent bodily harm—acted as a trigger for this hitherto unnoticed gene. The gene, once stimulated, distorted the chemical function of the cerebral cortex, and the result was the familiar progression of stigmata, hallucination, convulsion, death.

It was, of course, palpable nonsense. I did not tell him so. Pity restrained me. He needed me, he went on, to spread the word. I chided him, gently, on his phraseology. His response was impatient to the point of fury. I had to help, he insisted: my own expertise in linguistics dovetailed so neatly with his findings. The two of us, he said, could broadcast the key needed to unlock a cure. I allowed him to speak as long as he needed to, until the ambulance arrived and the receiver was quietly set down. Triage, in those days, was performed upon the spot.

The man's ravings were, of course, merely one more instance of the paranoia that marks the final hours of the victims of the plague. But, like all paranoid fantasies, his had some germ of truth in them, and it tantalized me. If we accept that the disease came into this world without phenomenal cause, another possibility remains. The disease is, I grant, born in the brain.

But it is not the product of any mechanism so vulgar as genetic coding. It is purely a product of the human mind.

I offer this as a message of hope. For if the plague had its origins in the human mind, might it not be fought by the same powers that called it forth? Tabitha had been "playing with the newspapers," her mother reported. So, this night, have I. I have before me the pages, already growing yellow, of the *I——Journal* in the first weeks of June. I visited the newspaper's offices last night, forced to break in with a wrecking bar. The streets of the town were still, but for someone singing in the upper floor above a nearby shop. The words of the song were unintelligible: only the tune came through, a wandering melody, almost familiar.

I have spread them out here before me, these pages from the morgue, my fingers trembling, the paper brittle, my breath unsteady in my chest. I read the stories there: they are the old familiar ones, always the same. Family burns in fire. Two held in convenience-store murder. Ultimatum issued over genocide. War in the Middle East. Old news: these portents and omens reduced to columns of fading ink.

I know, of course, the risk I am taking. I know only too well how fragile has been the chain of circumstances that has protected me from the infection. I listen even now to the stillness outside my window, and am awed by the hush there, and what it says to me of my own great fortune. It is a mournful silence, broken only by the eternal singing of the katydids. They call, as they always have, of the coming of winter: mournful, and yet somehow pleasant, as all melancholy is.

But before I digress again, I would report the last signifi-

cant item I have in my possession, and then I must go back
to my own work, which has been too long interrupted. The
information is this. In the later stages of the plague, the word
disappeared. Almost as if it were no longer necessary, the last
victims sickened, raved, and died without any visible sign of
illness. I have a theory, of course. And although there is no
means at my disposal to prove it even to my own satisfaction,
I am convinced it is true.

The word, whatever it meant, whatever form it took in
whatever language, was not the carrier of plague: not in any of
the ways we sought to understand. Understanding was beside
the point: for how could Tabitha, herself illiterate, have understood? The answer, plainly, is that she did not. I can imagine
the scene vividly, even now, as the child turned the pages of
the newspaper, rehearsing in her thoughts such anxieties as she
had heard adults around her voice over pages such as these.
Anxieties she did not understand, yet could not help but share:
anxieties that, for all she knew, were made of words. Words she
could not understand, but still she searched among them for
some clue, some answer to the riddle of her life.

Children are suggestible, reader. To go from fear of unintelligible danger to a physical expression of that fear required
only one word, any word, any arbitrary sequence of letters that
happened to come to her as she "read." That word, written
in blood on her features, took her to the hospital, confirming
all her fears—fears that conspired, after three days and nights
of what must have been pure, unremitting terror, to stop her
heart.

Do you doubt me, reader? What more would you have? Letters of fire across the sky? A voice speaking prophecy in your sleep? A look in the mirror at your own forehead? A list, per-haps, of the ways death can come to you, even as you read here, safe in your home?

What is it you want? The word?

I give you this, and then I must be gone. All you need is here before you—and the knowledge that what kills us now is any word at all, read in the belief that words can kill.

I know this now. I have been convinced for several days.

Ὁ Λογος!

Ὁ Λογος!

Ὁ Λογος!

MY FATHER'S HEART

My father's heart beats in a glass jar on the mantel, a steady flickering at the edge of my eye. I try to avoid it, but by dinnertime each night I'm staring. Beneath my gaze it pulses, and perhaps it turns a richer purple. From the jar I hear a low, dull, quick sound, persistent as a muffled watch.

You may know already what a small thing a heart is. Close your fist. Dig your nails into your palm two times quickly. Repeat. There it is. But my father's heart is large—fully as large as my head. The wide-mouth jar upon my mantelpiece once held a gallon of mayonnaise. Now, with the heart inside, it takes but two quarts of saline to brim it.

Atop the fluid, faint ripples shudder. Through them, I see the stubs of the aorta, vena cava, and the pulmonary vessels wave faintly, jerking. I tap the glass, and the tentacles withdraw; as suddenly as a slug surprised the whole mass shrinks, then slowly expands, and pulsates at its former size.

It has been a difficult possession. I am nervous about letting company near it. They might flick ashes in the jar, or jostle it. They might want to take it home. Vacations are, of course, out of the question. Whether the saline evaporates, or the heart in some way consumes it, I cannot say, but each day the level in the jar recedes, and I must top it off. Once each month the whole thing needs cleaning: I plop the beating mass out on the kitchen table—a few minutes in the air don't seem to bother it—rinse out the jar, and refill. The heart retakes its seat unruffled, seemingly oblivious, except for a slight flush around the coronary arteries, a slightly grander bulging on diastole.

But I tap the jar, and it mimes surprise: Don't tap, it says; don't tap. There is a dry, bleachy smell rising off the saline, and the faintest whiff of sweat.

It has learned the trick of propelling itself around the jar. The left ventricle twitches, a wave spurts from the descending aorta, and the whole mass rises from the bottom; a delicate pursing of the pulmonary arteries steers. I have found it at times spinning slowly, tootling an inaudible tune from the upbranching aortal pipes. On each rotation, it brings into view the scarification surrounding one collapsed and knotted vessel. It sees me staring, and with an abrupt spasm turns itself. The tubules wave at me. Go away, it says, go away.

I can't remember when it came into my possession. The question seems odd to me. When I stop and consider, of course I know that it must have come to me, on some day and in some place, but I feel it has always been with me. I know I had it when I went off to school, and carried it around from rented room to room, in and out of boxes for four years, and sometimes never a proper place to put it, hidden or exposed. My sophomore year it was a doorstop, but the gesture was transparent, to me and it, and there was bad blood on both sides.

Lately, I have felt the old antagonism resurfacing. I awake at night, and feel my own heart thudding wildly. I have fears—did I dine on botulism? am I growing bald?—and hear a low, dull chuckling from the other room. It is as mute as Adam when I see it by daylight, but I have suspicions of its nights. I have these past few evenings, about the hour of midnight, tried sneaking up on it with a flashlight. The beam reveals only a sodden lump of flesh, slumped and snoozing, a bubble hanging on the slack aortal lip. My own heart quiets at the sight, although at bottom I feel there lurks a lump of anger—sleeping, but alive.

I have raged at it of late: Leech, I cry: Bloodsucker. It burps clear saline in mild protest; innocence sits on every valve. I am not taken in. It has not been so many years since I have seen it raging in its turn, swollen to the size of a dirigible, as full of gas and fire, stopping traffic across four lanes of Sixth Avenue. A cab driver had refused to carry it: "I don't haul meat." I spent the balance of that day in terror, cradling the jar in my lap (we took a bus), looking into it each time the saline sloshed. It refused to look up.

At times—the oddest times—it has reared up inside its jar and reviled me. Ingrate, it cries. Weakling. Disappointment-to-me. I try to explain (I always try to explain), but the heart distends to twice its normal size. There is saline everywhere. I am afraid it will explode.

In an hour it is talking back at the small TV that sits beside its jar. It complains at the commercials. I keep my distance.

Once again I have awakened, and checking my pulse I find it slow, laboring, uneven. From the next room there is no sound. I snap on the light in the living room, and the heart starts, wrinkles into itself, and shields its blinking atria. Wake up, I tell it, knowing it is already awake, but I enjoy the violence in my voice too much to stop. Wake up. It is rubbing its bulging cheeks. I bring my face closer to the brine. Are you listening to me?

I have surprised it. No pirouetting, no calliope tunes: even the look of injured innocence is gone. It blinks up at me blankly, like a baby from a carriage, unsure. My own heart is racing.

Now I am here, I am not sure what to say. It won't wait long. Suddenly I am embarrassed, and, sensing this (it is uncannily acute), the heart starts to regain its buoyancy. Slyly, as if only at the whim of a current, it starts to rise through the fluid. I worry suddenly that it may break the surface, a gaping vein present itself an inch below my lips. I back away, mumble, "Just wanted to see you were all right."

Fantasies of revenge float through my mind all day. When I come home, I will slip it, jar and all, into the freezer. But does brine freeze? I could, while dusting, jostle it off its perch. The hearth is hard, the jar will shatter. It will flop about a minute or so, and then lie still. I am depressed when I arrive home. The key in the lock, the silence behind the door arrests me: what if something has happened? I fear the random violence of burglars.

One morning, I find the heart on the surface, lying on its

side, a froth of bubbles around it. It looks an unhealthy gray. I lift it from its fluid, and, unmindful of the wet, I cradle it against my chest. I croon soft words in its direction. It lifts an artery, and quivers.

A week passes, and all is well. It was singing this morning when I left for work, sporting with the bits of toast I fed it. The doctor has taken it off salt. I am cheerful, the morning air expansive in my chest. As I come home that night I am whistling.

It is as if nothing has happened. The heart turns its back ostentatiously as I enter. The television fills the room with cheers. As I try to speak, it waves an aorta impatiently for silence: a line drive into right field; one man comes home, then another; the last holds up at third. The crowd is wild; the heart is assiduously intent. I drop my briefcase on my bed and take a shower.

As the steam climbs up the glass, water gurgles about my feet, the sounds of the next room fade. The thudding in my ears is all my own; the jar on the mantelpiece is empty, a crust of salt at its bottom. Tomorrow, I tell myself, I will throw it away. And suddenly I am sobbing as if my heart will break.

CHARYBDIS

I shall from time to time continue this journal. It is true that I may not find an opportunity of transmitting it to the world, but I will not fail to make the endeavor. At the last moment I will enclose the MS in a bottle, and cast it within the sea. —MS. FOUND IN A BOTTLE

There is something I can't recall. It has a name, like *farther*, or *whom*, but these are wrong. It was in the dream that woke me this morning, we call it morning when I awaken here, but I couldn't remember the dream: only the shape of the word dissolving, a pair of lips parting, puckering *shh*. I told this to mission control, I don't know why. Maybe because the way they say "Good morning" annoys me: it's afternoon in Houston, and it's nothing you could call anything here. So I said there was something I couldn't remember, ate breakfast, and turned on the reader.

My coffee was cool by the time the reply came, breaking into their recitation of today's schedule: which system did I think it was in? Without pausing they returned to their list and read on. I lowered the gain, said "No, it's nothing real, it was in a dream. It sounds like *hips*, or maybe *warm*." I mixed more coffee and started a new story, one of Stern's mysteries: murder and incest, funerals, gunfire, somebody floating face-down.

Mission control muttered softly, static on the air. "Say again, *Prometheus?*" They hate to ask for confirmation, now the line of sight has stretched to twenty minutes. The distance makes communication between us strained, as I have come to suspect the lengthening pause between question and response. It makes their politeness sound too deliberate to be genuine. This is only an illusion, the effect of distance.

"It was in a dream," I told them, and looked from the reader out the port. Jupiter was off abeam, a featureless star so bright its light seems heavy. I can feel it in my eyes. Soon the image will spread, form a disc. I try to imagine what it will look like: a marble, a banded shooter, a catseye: I have seen pictures, but it will not be the same. There will be a salmon-colored eye-spot, which I'm looking forward to seeing. It was our mission's objective. At least it is something to wait for.

Return transmission was eight minutes late. "We've asked Dr. Hayford to discuss this with you. If you'd like." If I'd like: back at Houston, Hayford could have driven halfway home by now, leaving a string of words slung through the ether from mission control: I could no more shut him up than I could stop this ship. Since Stern and Peterson walked out on me, there's been a lot of empty deference on the airwaves, mostly incoming.

Dr. Hayford claims to know me better than my mother does, and this may be so, but I think he feels inadequate to this situation. "We've reviewed your transmission," he says. "I

gather it's not your nightmare. So I'm glad. You mentioned a
sound in this dream. That's a good sign. Would you like to talk
about it? I'll wait."

I told him if I remembered it I wouldn't have bothered
them in the first place, I didn't care about it anymore, let's quit
wasting time.

I let him think it was only a sound, but it was more: it was
a word.

HERE IS A list of mission control's euphemisms:

the burn
the event
the incident
the accident
the unfortunate [all of the above]
the spontaneous ignition
the midcourse miscorrection
the transorbital overenhancement. This one was my favor-
    ite, but the one they prefer is "the accident." I have started
    to ask them, "Which one?"

And they say I've lost my sense of humor.

I STILL NEED to explain. We slept afloat, adrift like tethered
fish, hugging ourselves to keep our arms from feeling awkward.
My mouth opens in my sleep, sometimes saliva wells around

my tongue, forms a sphere inside my mouth, and then I inhale it and wake, choking. I hack on the gob of spit, cough it out, and when I can breathe again I look around and see only dark, drifting shapes, I cannot remember who or where I am. I see Stern and Peterson afloat on their tethers; I hear them breathe, first one, then the other, a soft sound like water flowing into a drum. The ship cycles air, water; servos whine on and off around the hull, all these sounds are very close, and though I would wake immediately if they stopped, waking now gagging in the dark these sounds are stifling, and I think first I have awakened with a fever in my bedroom in my parents' home, I have heard the horn of a freighter on the lake; but then a window drifts in front of me, a light shines far beyond the pane, and I see stars, so thick they seem a solid mass, and the cabin walls could dissolve in an instant.

SICKENING PLUNGE THROUGH roaring; darkness; twitch at my belly the tether snapped; falling aft: down: we tumble together on the after bulkhead, Stern feet first and shouting, but the roar of the main engine drowns his voice, the darkness defeats us as we struggle. Peterson is motionless. The cockpit and controls now up against acceleration a dozen meters never meant to be climbed, I feel the distance stretching each second the ship leaps farther and faster ahead, leaving behind the fuel we need to get home. Banging my head against stanchions, losing my grip and slipping in the dark, alone, there is only one sound, and no progress upward: the ship is climbing away with us, and its gathering speed strips each moment out past measuring.

Suddenly there is light and I am blinded, blinking at the workbench I hug. Stern hangs from the opposite wall. We look up. A speaker squalls "... status ... cutoff ... manual": gibberish. I freeze, but Stern climbs again, barking more noise into air already too burdened to carry sense.

Nineteen minutes and some seconds pass before we can override the impulses that somehow opened the fuel system. Silence, and we fall freely again through space, faster now: I can feel the pace in my pulse. Peterson drifts forward through the cabin, his head trailing a pennant of blood.

NOW THAT THE cabin is empty, there is no reason to float around in bed any longer than the moment I awake: off tether, off to the head, breakfast, mission control like the morning news on the radio. I read more and more each day: deserts, dry gulches, buzzards circling. Jupiter stands off to starboard, brighter than before, and now I see a disc. I realize what I said in my first entry was a lie: I can't compare its size to anything we know, the head of a pin, an egg, my eye. If I had a penny, I could hold it to the glass and compare, but there's not a cent aboard, isn't that odd? I'm glad I can't: the comparison would show me nothing but a penny in my hand, and beside it, so far away I count the space in months, not miles: a planet. Its image is as clear as if etched on the glass, its satellites are perfect points of light beside it, all on a line, balancing. I envy them. I feel heavy and obtuse.

But I am weightless: an overhand pull swung me out of the cockpit and back into the cabin. Gone these five months and not once thought of cash, but I spent the rest of the afternoon tearing through Stern's and Peterson's effects, rifling the ship just to see. Not a cent.

MISSION CONTROL HAS many suggestions: about me, the ship, our mission. They are like bachelors babysitting. I sense fear in their omissions. "In theory . . ." they say, and skip ahead to speak of Jupiter. While I hang here listening, they weigh the orbits open to me there, and plan for my survival until rescue comes. They appear to have made a decision: they offer to make me a constellation, translate me into the sky with Io, Europa, and the rest. I am skeptical. It is not mission control that sets my course; it is ahead, Jupiter growing broader and brighter by degrees so small I never see the change, whom I must answer to. In practice, I doubt that I will have much to say in the matter.

There is one group that wants me to stop these recordings, and another wants them transmitted instead. A third thinks I should carry on, and one lonely man is horrified at the prospect. I suspect he knows what he is talking about, and wish he would shut up.

THE SHIP MOVES on, and forces me to choose. Here, the choices are simpler, the rules clearer: action, reaction; mass acting on mass; an object in motion tends to stay in motion, unless . . . But this kind of clarity is useless to me now, since I can see Jupiter clearly ahead, and know how all these equations balance, what answers they will come to: something very like a zero. I could crash there, of course; I could orbit it and wait for mission control; or I could crack the whip around it, shoot out in any direction I choose: how much more poignant to fly past Earth on my way out into darkness, moving too swiftly to say goodbye. I'd prefer to keep on the way I've come.

I prefer: in none of the equations for action, mass, and motion have I ever read a term for my capacity to choose. There are more things in heaven than in earth, I see that now. I am not in theory anymore; philosophy is not a dream. I am alive, that star behind me is the earth, and there is no "unless" in Jupiter. But there are choices.

WHILE THE BALANCE of its mind was disturbed, mission control brought my parents in to talk to me today. I mean that. I think they have taken leave of their senses, lost their marbles, gone off the deep end. My parents are in their nineties, and have not left the retirement home since I put them there ten years ago, and I do not visit often. Dad is aphasic; Mom talks, but how much is there to say? She asks me how my work is going, and I tell her, —Okay, and she says, brightly, —Good. Generally we leave it there, and spend our time more fruitfully on doctor's appointments, outings to the mall, the hazards of slippery floors. Once, when I told her I had just returned from Mars, confusion overwhelmed her. I pitied her then, with a generosity I needed desperately at the time. It is only recently I have come to wonder if her confusion is not after all a state of grace.

And now they've sent an air-conditioned sedan to fetch

them to the airstrip, bundled them on a NASA jet, trans-
shipped to Houston. Here. For a moment it seemed the radio
was eavesdropping on my childhood, the voice in the speaker
calling from the kitchen door, come in for supper, put on your
jacket, its getting late, time to come home. I shook my head,
wondering if this were one of Hayford's radio dramas, and I
the only one without a script, hearing her say, —Your father's
here. His voice saying, —Where is he? and then the cabin walls,
the stars outside, all fell away and I could see them in their
Florida clothing, their heads quivering on their delicate necks
as they turn to watch technicians passing, voices hurrying saying nothing they can understand.

"Get them off. Get them out of here. Take them home."

I cut the connection.

I HAVE BEEN floating here in silence since, thinking of my
alternatives, to stop at Jupiter or travel on: the journey outward, into silence so thick as to become something: a pressure, a presence here with me. As weight surrounds a mass,
so silence would fill the air around me, falling in, rising from
blood rustling in my ears to become a whisper, a word spoken,
a cry, the roar of burning and finally the crash of everything
that falls. Beyond Pluto, silence would be more than absence
of speech: even zero has meaning, but what is zero taken to an
infinite power? And on what fingers do I count it? Though I
could hear the singing of the spheres, see colors off the spec-
trum, touch nothing: how could I tell? and whom?

I reach up and touch my ears: they are cool. I try to trace
their infoldings with my finger, picture the pattern there, but

my mind won't follow: *pinna, auricle*, these words drift through my thoughts, and I don't know where I learned them, or how they might help me in the silence beyond Jupiter. I only know that between cool flesh and colder vacuum, I will have my hands full. I am Jupiter-bound.

But by how long a chain?

STERN AND PETERSON left in that order, on successive days. The initiative was Stern's. We did not talk much in the days following the burn. At first, I attributed this to simple shock, and fear for our survival. Conversation seemed at first a burden, then a risk. But just as we no longer sensed our new velocity once acceleration ceased, so our increased risk became a piece with the fears we'd shared since liftoff and before. Still we found it hard to talk, even to meet each others' eyes: as if the sudden return to free fall, the leap from acceleration to silence, had shaken something loose and left us trying to remember how to talk.

Stern started mumbling after a week, odd things, as if he thought we wouldn't hear: "elucidate," "supernal," "ineluctable." He prowled like a pregnant cat, carrying objects to and from the hold: I remember his back receding through the hatch, shoulders hunched and holding something precious: a hand-vacuum, binoculars, a hair-dryer. On a Monday I heard him mutter "Terra matter," and on a Tuesday he was gone. He left in the lander, leaving us its portable seismometer and a set of digging tools, a deeper silence, and then the voice of mission control, advising us of a change of plans.

He left at night. The whine of servomotors woke me and

Peterson to wonder why the hold had opened, and where was Stern, and then, befuddled, why the hold-hatch was dogged: through the deadlight we saw nothing, then stars burning in vacuum, and we understood, slowly, why the hatch wouldn't open, why we were locked in, and as we floated there, feeling like children at a bedroom door, Peterson croaked "Wait"—to Stern, to himself or no one—concussion echoed through our hands, knees, noses, whatever touched metal, and the hold was filled with fog, swirling, clearing: empty.

We tracked Stern by the light of his main engine until he faded in the stars, and then by radar. He dropped rapidly astern, but before we lost him we learned his trajectory. He would fall into the sun sometime in May.

Naturally Peterson was hurt. He and Stern had trained together, shared Naval Academy ties and a series of back-yard barbecues in Houston, of which there is still a Polaroid taped over the galley microwave: two men, two women, the men wearing dark glasses, the women with the loopy shut-eyed look that comes from too much sun and a fast shutter. Their arms are mostly hidden: here and there a hand appears, disjointed beside someone's neck. There is no indication who took the picture, but in my imagination I am the photographer, and I think this prevents my tearing it up. I am surprised Peterson did not take it with him: it was Stern's second wife, but Peterson's first.

JUPITER WAS ACTIVE on the decameter band this afternoon, crackling and hissing like a witch and her cauldron. I piped it back into the hold all day while I worked there on one of the instrument packages. I have been dreaming again, a nightmare in which I am unable to awake. This makes the silence in the ship nerve-wracking: hence Jupiter. It reminds me of surf, and the hold can be my boathouse, my Ogygya. I may leave the radio on tonight, a mood record, like those used in nurseries to lull the babies with big soft noises—but something stops me. This is not a record.

At the suggestion of mission control, who want one instrument package sent to Io in place of the lost lander, I work in the lighted hold, holding on to handgrips with my toes as I modify the contents of the capsules—three featureless shells. They shine in the floodlights, smooth as pills rolling under your tongue, as hard to hold on to; so blandly polished their scale is as hard to grasp as their surfaces: from across the hold they can look as small as BBs, and the hold no wider than a mailing tube; sometimes they could be worlds, and at the hold-hatch I cling to the top of a well dropped down from heaven. The weightlessness does this.

I prefer to work inside them, where I curl comfortably. Their brushed-metal interiors give back no reflections (outside, the distortions are immense), only a dim shape that moves with me in the corner of my eye. Jupiter's speechless hissing comforts me then, a voice tongueless as a radio wave. But I know when the cabin lights cycle off tonight and I float to sleep, I will not have the courage to keep a radio turned on in this ship. I possess already—perhaps I have dreamed it—a sense of how it will be when I wake suddenly to Jupiter's voice pronouncing words, whole sentences, my name. I have enough trouble with my dream.

In my dream I am Peterson, or with him in his suit, and we

are looking back at me, at the ship, as Peterson drifts away. His tether gone or never connected, tumbling through the stars revolving, looking out, looking back, we do not see my face in the cockpit window. In my dream I know the ship is deserted, and although it is I who have left it, I feel abandoned. Lights burn in every port along its length, and every port shows empty in the light. The hold stands open, open on a two-car garage, lined with lawn mowers, ladders. The cars are gone. Oil gleams darkly from the center of the floor, unreflecting. I change my mind. I am too sad, too tired or sick or small to go, and I want to turn back, but it is too late.

He took no means of rescue with him. Once he stepped outside the airlock unattached, once he jumped, he was committed. I think he knew the limits of his resolve, and surrendered himself to physical law before he could recant. In my dream, I open my mouth to speak but I cannot. There is no air. Tears puddle in my eyes but won't fall. The absence of air, the suspension of gravity: I recognize these things. They return to me, as if I knew them once but long ago forgot. Breath, weight, those are spells finally broken, exceptions now set aside. This is real.

And only when I pass beyond denying this can I awake and remember the rest of the story.

I don't know what woke me, the night Peterson left. The operation of the airlock is almost silent, and unless he made some sound, I cannot explain how I came to witness his leap of faith. I suspect he did signal me, deliberately, banging a wrench against a bulkhead until he saw me move, and then he turned to the open hatch, to crouch and spring. He was not far when I reached a porthole.

When I saw a spacesuit in free fall beside us, I turned to summon Peterson, to tell him there was a man out there, should we shoot a line? There was something terrifying about the absence of an umbilical between the suited figure and the ship: my mind refused to supply the missing connection. I was afraid to look behind me. Long seconds passed, in which the image of a human form, tumbling in somersaults, shrank. I floated, I froze, I gave no thought to rescue, to fear or pity, to anything but the gradual diminution of the figure, until I recognized his waving arms, and remembered the man they signified: I bolted overhand—away from the airlock, my eyes clenched shut. Blind momentum carried me to the cockpit, and the radio.

His frequency was full of speech when I found it. A sob rocked the room before I could back off the gain, and then, gasping, Help me, and, I'm sorry.

I sat in my couch and looked out the windshield, where the galaxy slanted across the ecliptic, between Gemini and Orion. I tried to find the lines between the stars that make a pair of twins, a hunter, but the figures crumbled, forming trapezoids, triangles, and finally single stars burning red, blue, gold at the bottom of the black.

"What's wrong?"

Nothing moved.

"What is it?"

Only stars far away, and his voice coursing on unnoticing, his remorse weighting me, and I stayed and watched the stars beyond the screen and listened, as if the voice were a lost memory, a dead child, a dream.

And even when I moved to ask the proper questions, he did

not respond. I knew his receiver was finally *Off*, and it didn't matter. I saw nothing when I returned to the cabin port, but his voice remained, lingering in the radio, where it cried and cried. His signal followed, fading too slowly, for hours: time enough to return, and return, to the sorrow and the emptiness. He thought it was a trick, an exercise, a game, but he was wrong it's only empty space and I'm sorry. Help me.

I switched it off.

SO I AM alone. Mission control approached me later with a surprising delicacy, a care to avoid certain words. Perhaps my inaction on Peterson's behalf disturbed them: or perhaps out of the three they had most expected me to jump. They may no longer feel sure of whom they're dealing with, and their delicacy is the caution demanded by a dawning sense of ignorance. Perhaps they no longer think me trustworthy. I think when they failed to take this up with me, they stopped being entirely candid.

THE SILENCE HAS burrowed deep into my dreams. In them, human forms flash by, and I see their faces turning as they pass, their lips moving, forming one word. Always it is the same word, but the sound I hear is not speech, nor is it ever the same. One figure passes, my mother, who tells me it is a car's horn honking. My physics teacher says it is a hissing fire, a gas jet. To my dead brother, it is the sound of stones dropped in deep water. I call after them, but can make no sound at all until

I wake, tangled in my sleep-tether, whispering "Wait" into an empty cabin.

I wake from dreams into memories, moments long submerged resurfacing. Standing shivering by a swimming pool, my shadow beside me on the concrete a thin wavering, listening as an instructor down a line of slick-skinned children gave a command, and all down the line they flung themselves into the water. I remember watching a silver bubble burst and quiver above me, shimmering into the quicksilver sky, and then the ecstatic inrushing of water as if I too were rising.

Years later, in school I learned about specific gravity, the opposing forces of air and water, how the nature of air is to rise, how any solid body, even if of rock, can reach its equilibrium and float—in air, if need be, if air be dense enough. And I thought: This is why I like science; and I felt once more the possibility of rising. But going into space taught me again. I unlearned, and science is a consolation only to the ignorant.

CONSIDER THE NAMES of the ships: *Mercury*, *Gemini*, *Apollo*; *Ares*, where I earned my wings, and now *Prometheus*. Think how the missions lived up to their names: *Mercury*, an aery theft of thunder from the Soviets; *Apollo*, to a chaste sister giving sacrifice by fire; *Ares*, and the terror it brought us to. God save the man who rides on *Kronos*.

THE COMPUTER IS my timekeeper, it is my courier and my library. It stores in its memory the pages I call up on the screen.

For my collection I chose Shakespeare, Melville, the old myths. My crewmates left their libraries with me: Stern loved mysteries; Peterson was more a western man.

I spend hours at the screen now, and though I am grateful for the machine, it leaves me skeptical. I wish often for the weight, or at least the solidity, of a book, instead of the image of words on glass. The transience of the picture worries me, and I have caught myself calling back earlier pages, comparing them to my own memory to see if the text has been altered by the computer's traffic with so much other information. Sometimes, I am tantalized by a suspicion—surely that word was not *noses*, but something starting with a *g*; and that was *cave*, not *save*; not *screen*, but— I catch myself, and read on.

MISSION CONTROL WANTS me to look at the communications antenna, which is a paraboloidal dish big enough for a man to lie in. Servomotors aim it constantly toward mission control, so the dish faces back the way I've come, my Janus. They sound more worried than usual back in Houston, and although it could easily be an act, put on for reasons I may no longer guess, it seems they really are having trouble understanding. Somewhere in the system something's wrong, but at their end or mine no one can tell: they want me to go outside and see if, perhaps, something grossly physical (and therefore beyond their power to control) has come unhinged. They sound desperate.

I switch on the aft external video and eye the dish. It eyes me back, pointed steadily at Earth, which is a white star off to port and well astern. The dish looks fine to me, I tell them, and wait. No, they insist, someone there believes a meteor may have knocked the antenna off focus: I must go see for myself. Without waiting for my reply, they begin to outline the procedure, the tools I will need, the complicated route along the ship's back, how I must unhook my tether to clear the dish. Under Houston's control, the inner airlock door slowly opens to receive me.

I listen as the voice clips through the cockpit speakers, each syllable enunciated so sharply it stands alone. They are giving me instructions. I am not paying attention. Jupiter has crept into the forward section of the windshield, striped and swirling, closer, and suddenly the pattern I have watched for weeks snaps, and as if a picture has jumped off a printed page and rolled into my lap I see the planet's marblings turn, and turn into clouds, winds: weather. It is a place, not a pattern. The red spot stands dead center, a catseye blinking back at me. I feel exposed.

"Wait a minute." I speak before I can catch myself. "This isn't—" The airlock door waits, open like a mouth. I know now where I have heard all this before. My breath is taken away by the stupidity of the ploy. Do they think because I am out here I cannot remember old movies? Is no one back there capable of original thought?

Am I?

IN THE FORTY minutes before they could respond, I watched Jupiter turn ahead: the red spot lay obliquely now; sleepily askance, it eyed the insertion point for the orbit I must assume if mission control's plan to rescue the ship is to succeed. But it was the opening of the airlock door that reminded me: they can fire the engines for the braking maneuver just as well from Houston as I can here; better. How much better? How have they calculated my unreliability by now? How large is that factor in their equations? How does it balance with the safety of the ship?

I know how to balance an equation.

I ponder now how much of their talk has been of rescuing the ship, not me. Did they think an omission like that would pass me by?

I ask the computer: Is there enough fuel left to shake me from the dish and still save the ship at Jupiter? The computer gives the figures: fuel for the braking burn and some to spare. I stare at the screen, wondering if the answers are reliable, wondering if even now mission control is feeding me false data. Time elapsed from last transmission stands at 08:20, 21, 22. I am safe for thirty-one more minutes. And then? How much longer before they think up some subtler stratagem? If they grow desperate enough, will they simply open the outer airlock door?

The voice of mission control courses on, urging me to check the seals on my cuffs. Hurrying, I pull the spacesuit from its locker. High in my chest I feel the seconds ticking.

EMPTY SPACE. STARS swarming in: I heard them humming in my headphones. I closed my eyes: darkness, stars shining through. I put my hands to my eyes, but the gloves fell flat on my faceplate. My head afloat in its helmet, sweat stung my eyes; I leaned my skull against the globe and through the glass heard nothing. No: there, between Castor and Capella, something flashed, faded, flashed again. Something whispered in my ear. Something reflected the sun as it tumbled. "Peterson," I whispered, and it flashed. I watched, and the light neither grew nor faded, nor moved against the stars. It was following.

I turned and held hard to the ship, and though I felt the light flash behind me, counting its rhythm against my pulse I crawled along the hull. I passed portholes through which I saw the cabin, lighted and calm, where objects waited as if left by someone else. I reached the knot where I had spliced Peterson's tether to mine. I passed over lettering painted on the hull: signs and insignias lay like shells on the seafloor, like fossils in rock. I waited for one of them to move.

When I reached the dish I turned to look. There was the lander hovering, there was Peterson's mummified face pressed close to mine, gibbering in his helmet—for a moment every direction was down.

Then there was nothing, just my tether trailing back to the open hatchway, and the slow revolution of stars.

The dish was fine. I crawled around it, gripping the tripod that held the antenna at its focus, and my shadow fell across its face. Radio traffic was passing through my body, my computer talking to theirs, and probably them talking to me, spinning out their story; static. I gripped the antenna boom and stared at it: instructions for removal, the NASA insignia, but no clue, no hard fact explaining what was going wrong between us: nothing.

Nothing: I had come to the end of my tether and found—I

turned and faced the flashing following me: nothing. Only the on and off of it, on and off. Static; and in my helmet, my breath, and the sound of swallowing.

I reached for the antenna to tear it off, to do away with mission control and their instructions. Fools or liars, I can no longer tell the difference: everything they say sounds false, devoid of sense; or in this void of sense, nothing they can say will help. It does not matter. But as I reached up I looked and saw the flash, fade, and flash again.

"No," I said, and it vanished. No: and it never reappeared.

No. I would not rip out my tongue for mission control.

I went inside and overrode antenna guidance, steered it away from Earth. Mission control faded in midsentence like a dream. I swiveled the dish a hundred eighty degrees in azimuth, faced it forward until the decameter hiss of Jupiter filled the room.

I KEEP THE radio on, now the time is free for me to fill, metered only by the tripping in my chest. I have shorted out the cycle on the cabin lights and gone to manual. Sometimes, I work in the hold, removing instruments from one of the capsules. The instruments are useless to me now; I want the shell. Sometimes, on ship's radio, I transmit. Music. I have not spoken yet. Jupiter has not answered. It grows oblate ahead, and I wait for word.

AHEAD HAS BECOME beneath.

We thread through satellites too fast to read Europa's scars, past Io's peacock eyes, the radio snarling static from the radiation belts. We dive down deep, into Jupiter's sphere now filling the sky, now out of sky we fall. A horizon encircles us, flattens to a wall we climb, a ceiling we cling to, striped with fire, clay, cream, rust, slate, straw, snow. I doubt my calculations, doubt the sense of reckoning with anything this huge. The whole world hangs above, a few dim stars below. We soar or swim, I do not know. We must be close enough to see, or it was all for nothing. I will have all or nothing.

The computer chatters beside me, parroting the terms I fed it weeks ago, but my eyes are pulled from its screen out past our bows, to the end of the broad brown ridge of cloud we follow, ahead where darkness rises. It sweeps up and over us in a second and the sun is gone: the aft camera shows a rim of red stretching from horizon to horizon, then, dizzying, the computer swivels the ship to face the sunset where light filters like an infection deep into the planet's limb, until Jupiter seems lit from within by fevers, forges; moonsglow falls ashen on cloudtops. The computer throws a series of numbers across its screen, countdown glowing green in the darkened cabin, gleaming across my knuckles where they grip the armrests, and as the numbers reach zero and turn to the word *Ignition* we have ignition and the world is flattened.

OUR ORBIT IS low, in more than secular decay, mission control would have said, leaving me to wonder how much weight to give which meaning of the word.

I am grateful already for the silence they finally surrendered me: I no longer hear their echo mocking in my ears. Only Jupiter fills them now, the voice proper to the scene I see, if only I could fit the sounds to sight and make some sense of both, strain an answer from the chaos below. I need new words for what I see, and as we pass low over the cloudtops, the hazy regions where my decaying course will drop me, spiral me down in a week or a month, I don't care to calculate, somewhere in my chest I sense the suspension—above or below—of a crushing weight.

JUPITER SPEAKS SYLLABLES, sibilants, subsides. I no longer need direct the antenna: the sound seems to pierce the cabin walls, rising from the chaos below. I have broadcast nothing since we entered orbit, but hourly I feel silence grow gravid around me. I have moved Stern's couch from the cockpit, and fitted it in the empty capsule.

Below, finally, it spreads over the pale horizon and advances: the Great Red Spot I called it, but now I see only a tide of red swallowing everything. The nose of the ship bleeds pink, the light in the cabin suffuses dim red. We have arrived, and nothing is as I expected. Spot? A continent swirls below me, the skin of a world stripped off and spread still dripping across the flanks of Jupiter. I look down and see clouds churn, swallowing, the whole so huge we seem to slow in our passage, or else the ship is drawn toward the shadowed hollow at the center.

THE HOLLOW PASSES off our starboard wingtip, and leaves me wondering what to call it now that I have seen: a cyclone, monsoon, typhoon—metavortex to the dozens I see spun off and shattered below, as much in size to them as they are like a hurricane. No. I do not know. This storm will blow for a million years, as it has blown since before a man worked stone, learned fire, or sketched the shadow of his hand against a cave wall. And at its center, a hazy depth, calm blue, blue as eyes, leading in. I must see closer.

The radio is silent.

IT CHANGES HUE with every revolution: now an ember, now a rose, a sore, the underside of my tongue.

We pass far north of it on one orbit, and it lies on the horizon like the glow of a city.

We pass over its center, and the dark center, its rim raised, is a caldera. Etna, I think: Olympus. My chest aches. Ten years ago I stared down the throat of Olympus Mons on Mars, alone at the controls of a ship much like this, while Stern descended to the surface, and returned with eight charred bodies, five women and three men, my crewmates. Through twenty orbits returning like a tongue to a broken tooth I looked down, I wanted to see, there, on a piece of soil irrevocably so, the place where the rocks had burnt blacker, the shards of the ship shining. I looked down, fearing to see the flame of the lander ascending, dreading the quiet at our reunion, a stillness still unbroken.

Now I see. I look down on the eye of the storm, and though the resemblance is uncanny I feel nothing: I am careful not to move: a word was balanced within me, but down the vortex I see nothing. A drop of water drifts before my eyes. In it I see reflected all the colors that are on Jupiter. I find I have been sobbing.

It drifts away, and I sleep, undreaming. When I wake my chest feels emptied, the cabin is filled with light, and I lie quiet.

I SPENT THIS day at the telescope, watching the surface, setting up a trajectory on the computer. I returned to the instrument capsule, the hollow shell of it, and began again, piling on the couch inside it some things I should jettison: the program manuals, two photographs, some tools. Each thing suggested a dozen more alike in their absurdity, their profanation of this place, and then I worked through a time that passed unnoticed, until I found the capsule almost full and the hold, the cabin, the cockpit stripped, a free space almost like the one outside, bounded only by these featureless walls, this steel painted white. I had not thought the shell would hold so much.

I heard it then at last, in the silence I have heard more clearly since I left the earth behind: I heard the word I came so far to learn.

I heard no signal, saw no blinding flash; the heavens did not open, nor the rocks: but as I fitted in the sphere a single shoe— lost half of a pair once made by Converse but the name no longer matters—only now that all these things are gone and my world is empty do I understand: nothing. Nothing: in a world of lies, the only word that tells the whole unholy truth. It was before my beginning, it waits beyond my end. It inhabits every word I have recorded here but these words too are nothing. Only nothing: and nothing is a word and nothing more.

All or nothing: I threw into the capsule the object I held in my hand, but before I seal them all inside I must complete my mission: all or nothing.

I have not dismantled the ship: I need it to live in until I die. But I will make an exception now, and open the panel where the computer's memory lies. On the hard drives, wheels within wheels, the many million words: they all must go. Drive follows drive into the capsule, until only one remains, still spinning: listen. I will not touch it. I can jettison the rest, drop every trace of Earth, every memory of mission control into the eye, and cleanse myself of the last of my earthly inheritance. And on the necessary air, food, fuel, and water, and this small store of words, my own, await my story's end.

IN THE ECHOING emptiness left in the ship I watch and I wonder as the capsule drops shining away, sun lighting its limb, a crescent moon, Diana, what I would see and what hear had I gone, as it sounds down into the eye of the storm darkly blue with the baying of God's great hounds. I see the capsule turn in its fall, a slow dreaming spin, a top's sleeping. I see its porthole come round, a flash in the sun blinking back at me.

What would I see? This ship, winged V, Nike, Styxdaughter, Zeus-attending. No more. The noise of our fall would grow, swell, soaring. Down faster now, through thin keening, clouds whipping: it hazes a minute and I fear it lost. Then again suddenly smaller it flashes falling silver into the indigo center, one bright swimming in violet falling and deeper. The sound would be shaking now as it slows, glowing dull red from the wind, the action of sounding. Weight grows on it, pound on pounding, and I think of a bubble in water unsinking and see: it is gone. See no splash. Silent.

AURORA

Then will I also confess unto thee that thine own right
hand can save thee. —JOB 40:14

The ice falls, swept by time and what first impulse I do
not know, only that now it falls, free in its falling, the
drift of it I envy. See it roll. See the breaking of it, ice on ice, the
brightness of it breaking in the twilight, breaking into shards,
into dust, into shining, into a haze of light, into darkness: see
it vanish.

And on the Ring I only do not break. I do not vanish: I ride
the wheel of it, arms out against the fall. No glittering shards of
me disperse. My heart is solid inside me, a steady turning.

I cannot remember when this was not so.

I KNOW THE ice. I know the darkness north and south, I know
the great bulk of Saturn below. I know *Aurora* rising to meet me
in her time. Only myself I do not know.

Of myself, I see only fragments. There is my auger, the sharp point of me, glittering at end like ice, scoured by ice and harder. There are my arms: these thin rods of titanium, articulate and shining, hooked at end with tungsten claws. The rest I do not see, and know only by a sensation I cannot describe: a dull vibration in the frame of me. There are doors: I shrug and they open for ice. And beyond the doors, a chamber where ice is melted, though I feel no heat; only the opening of valves. There are valves, and motors to drive them; nozzles where I vent off meltwater, a cloud of light returning to the Ring. And at my heart a gyroscope revolves, so finely tuned to falling that I cannot feel it, unless I turn against the fall.

In the hollow that is most of me, the heavy elements of my refining linger. I know their names, and the weights of them: how they answer to Saturn by falling, to the call that comes louder as they press within me, but still we fall no faster, I do not feel them, I have no sight or taste or touch of them: only their heft, the mass that binds me still more strongly to the Ring, until *Aurora* comes, and I am set out again among the ice.

Aurora always comes. What signals her I do not know. So much is out of my control.

I do not sleep.

I know *sleep*: it is in the motion of the ice that falls around me: falls, and does not change. It is in the falling of us all—in the ice adrift, in the darkness where we fall, the darkness there that draws me on but never into Saturn, only falling, the ice and I, toward *sleep* that never comes. It is one of those words from the darkness within me, words like *hope*, like *pain*, like *love*, one of the words that falls nowhere.

I sense other words in the darkness, words I cannot hear. I only feel them echo in the hollow within me. They jar this voice that speaks distinctly in my thoughts—disturb it, as the ice around me jostles in its fall. They tell me that, in some other life I cannot imagine, in some time I cannot recall, I was not as I am now.

THERE IS A voice in me that is not mine. It is all I hear between me and the Ring. The voice whispers: I am two point nine seven nine oh hours into this revolution; my target is at range three eight point oh six four; my payload is at thirty-five percent.

It occupies my thoughts. It keeps the silence from entering. It carries me, as ceaselessly as time, as irresistibly as the Ring itself sweeps onward. I feel myself within it falling, unable to ignore it, unable to reply.

I think sometimes it speaks to keep me from thinking.

Vision also intercedes between me and the ice, lights that are to my mind's eye as the voice is to my thoughts: in a violet line against the stars my target shows eight ragged peaks at wavelengths of so many nanometers. These are the signs of uranium, the voice tells me.

In the darkness, in the silence, the voice and the visions, they comfort me.

Saturn has voices; the Ring and the darkness have voices too: they chorus on some sense that once was hearing. At Saturn's core a murmur speaks of time; above its poles, electrons wail in their spiraling fall. From the darkness, a dim hissing: this is the voice of the stars.

And once each revolution I hear the Ring itself awake into the sun. It calls, in a cadence that pulses, waking echoes in the hollow within me, echoes that might be words: words like *sorrow*, like *loss*; but the voice inside me whispers *static discharge, coulombs, hertz*: the voices of the Ring are hushed, the echoes die away, and I am comforted.

But still, each revolution, at the pulsing of the ice, in a hollow inside me something opens. In the dull drum of me something beats, as though trapped and calling, the note of it fading, and then only silence, and within me the sound of a motor whining briefly, venting ice.

ONE BY ONE, the moons draw near. In my frame I feel them: Iapetus and Phoebe, Dione and Tethys, Rhea, and the largest one, orange and featureless in my long-range vision. I know their names, I do not know how. In my frame a yearning rises, but it is not for them. For something like them, but what I cannot say. I long for some great fall. Not into Saturn, not into the night that holds us all, but into what I cannot say: into something that is not the Ring, something distant and solid, like the moons. Like myself.

Saturn is not solid: the voice tells me so, feeding me data: the pressure there so many millibars, the composition so much of ammonia, free hydrogen, water-ice. The temperature is so many degrees Kelvin, and I know that is cold, although here in the Ring the ice is colder. But what a millibar is, what once was fractured into thousands, I cannot say, nor what was Kelvin before it became a thing of degrees. Nor how I know a *milli* is a thousandth, or a *degree* a thing of crumbling.

Ammonia, water: I know these. These are the constituents
of ice. I know, too, that I need them to survive: they feed me,
in some way I know only from the hunger that I feel for them.
And though I do not taste them, I know them with the inti-
macy hunger brings. I see them. I hear them always calling
from the Ring, from the ice I grapple, from the shining spray
I vent, prismatic in the sun, a glory I fall through as it fades,
vanishing, returned into the Ring.

So much is vanishing here. Only I do not: I remain, the
moons' stress in my frame telling me only I am solid. And
echoes, telling me I am a thing of—echoes.

I CANNOT SEE the sun. I have tried, but there is a command
in me that will not let me look. The voice tells me my cameras cannot stand the light: an instant, and I would be blind,
and without vision I cannot mine the ice. And without ice, it
tells me, my life will be an endless fall through hunger: a fall
through time made merciless by darkness, through darkness
unbroken by change.

But I have tried. I do not know why. Only that the way
the sunlight breaks upon the ice—the brilliance of it flashing
here, where seeing and vanishing are one; this poignancy I
cannot capture, though it touches me each instant as I turn,
and turn, and fall upon the Ring: all of this, and what more
I cannot say because it comes from what within me I do
not know—all of this draws me, despite all warning, to look
toward the sun.

I cannot. My cameras swivel, focus, range and shift all
out of my control, and never in all the revolutions of the

Ring have they let me see what lies there, where shadows fall from.

But still I want to see.

OUT OF THE A Ring, bright against the Division, falling now into the B Ring and toward me, *Aurora* comes. I see her engines flare: flakes of ice vanishing in bright vapor she brakes, nearing now: beside me, docking: our collars match, mate, our systems mesh, and once again she is here.

From connections I cannot feel *Aurora*'s presence floods through me, lights and echoing voices not my own flow in. My sensors detune, the stars dim, and before the new instructions seat themselves, I know that once again I am about to remember.

But then the sun flickers, the sky is black again so soon I cannot remember what color it was; the bulk of *Aurora* eclipses the stars, the new instructions execute, and the voice in me returns.

It is speaking of iridium. It has a warbling note, four peaks on the spectral graph.

I cannot remember what I remembered. For one brief moment's inward fall I know that in a moment more I will forget I remembered at all, and now only the dim shiver, low in my empty hold.

I DO NOT know the nature of my thoughts. Where do they come from? Where do they go? Are they saved or are they lost?

Does *Aurora* hear them, or something beyond *Aurora*? I cannot say. I know only that to me they are irrevocable: I think them, and they vanish. This is the nature of the Ring.

But if I could recall these words, hear them once again above the voice that distracts me, I might know what it is that pains me. But now *Aurora* signals her departure, and with a rupture, with pain, the channels break, the valves seal, collars spin, decouple. Her jets flare in the sun and she is gone.

I watch, hoping to learn where she goes. The flame of her engines lifts her above the Ringplane and out, climbing, brilliant again against the Division, then over the A Ring and dwindling, the shape of her lost below resolution, the flame finally below my cameras' threshold and I am falling.

I do not know where these words go. They vanish from me, into darkness. And like the Ring, their vanishing is endless.

I FALL THROUGH darkness, the sun eclipsed by Saturn's huge night. Along the Ring, a dim bridge into light, I listen, urgent after iridium. I grapple ice loud with it, auger in. It breaks, pieces fall away. I gather them, feed them into me. My frame rings loudly with their impact within.

I gather all but one: it has flown farther, up out of the Ring. I follow, clamber, carom, climb up into spaces where ice is scant. And there, my limbs go sluggish.

It is always like this. There is a command within me: it will not let me too far from the Ring: it outweighs even the hunger for ice. Off the Ring, the voice tells me, the emptiness is deadly: ten hours without ice and my systems fail. So when I try to climb I am given heaviness, a reluctance that would be *fear* but it does not belong to me. I feel it imposed, a command that does not need a voice: it has my limbs in its control, my strength its hostage.

And to oppose it I am given only hunger.

Caught between the heaviness and hunger I stop, still drifting out.

Here above the Ringplane, a kilometer of emptiness below me, I circle with the Ring, a ghost off a ghost-road through darkness. Uneasy, I yearn for the Ring. Under the prompting of the voice, I thrust: I feel the spray of vapor oppose my momentum, but it is too weak: soon it sputters, it tails off, my tank is empty, and I am drifting. Anxious now I listen, but for a long time the voice within me, intent on the Ring, is silent.

Then a slow number speaks itself. I am drifting far out, far into stillness, and even the voice is still.

Far from the Ring I am drifting, helpless to control my flight. In the emptiness here, my horizon opens. Space is everywhere. It seems to open even into me. In the silence, heedless for once of ice, my cameras drift. The voice is still; the echoes are still as well. Only these thoughts remain, loud and uncontrollable.

Without warning, the Ring below bursts into light. The ice awakens, the Ring's chorus pulses; slowly, the sound fades away.

When the silence returns, light lies everywhere around me, and still the voice is silent. The silence is harrowing. The light is merciless. The transparency of space appalls me. Below, Saturn's body is alive: I see each storm as it uncoils, each uneasy surge of ice-fog, and everywhere the sheer terror of wind. And on the Ring I see the multitudes of the ice, each in its singular-

ity distinct, each in its moment of flashing as sharp, as ephem-
eral as pain. It is all here, and I am here in it, solid, drifting, and
strange. It is as though I have never seen this before.

Far ahead in the darkness, something hovering over the
Ring catches the light of the sun. Its graph is dim, peaked in
a pattern I have never seen. The voice says nothing. Without it, I am helpless to identify. But something inside me has
started to clamor. With an effort, I swivel the long-range camera forward.

At the limits of resolution, it shows me a cylinder spinning
slowly, end over end. A narrow neck. The ungainly growth of a
head. I see a pair of arms: thin, articulate, and hooked at end.
It drifts through emptiness, even farther from the Ring than I
have come. It falls, flashing in the sun, its arms held out against
the fall.

Abruptly, the voice returns. It tells me we are falling; in two
point nine oh two hours we will return to the Ring, entering at a relative velocity of so many meters per second: three
point seven encounters with ice of average mass will disperse
the polar vector of our speed. We are saved.

I am not listening. I am struggling not to listen. I am struggling to hold on to my cameras, struggling to hold the silence,
struggling to remember what I have seen; struggling against
the voice, against the ice, against the Ring, against the fall back
into sleep. I am falling.

In the depths of my hold, as I turn to face the Ring, as I ready
my arms for ice, like a bad bearing starting to break down, like
an ingot working loose, something shudders against the fall.
The echoes inside me are loud.

I AM PLAGUED by double vision. My cameras, compelled, seek ice. They are bound to iridium, to measuring vectors of collision and capture, as my thoughts are bound to the Ring and the voice. But a *memory* has survived in me, a silence I wedge between us. In instants that pass almost before I can grasp them, I can see.

I cannot look. But in glimpses left to me, past the graph, through the tumbling ice, in the spaces between the words, I remember, and I watch for the other I saw.

Ahead it drifts, high above the Ring. But as I watch it is falling back into the ice, rolling in a slow helpless fall. In a rush it vanishes, lost in the sweep of the Ring far ahead and I am left aching, as if to an echo of impact.

But abruptly below the Ring I see it again, reaching out into the darkness against the stars of Virgo. Past Spica it flashes, tumbling faster now. An arm is waving in my direction; light glints off a lens as it swivels my way.

It is calling me to follow.

ON ANOTHER REVOLUTION I see it rise again out of the Ring before me. On its long outward reach, as it dwindles to a star it seems to slow; it seems to stop; *it is not falling*. It is motionless against the stars. I am aching with envy.

I know it must be falling.

It hangs, as if motionless, but holds its station, high above and far ahead. It is falling. I stare at it, my cameras resisting commands to turn to the ice. I am fascinated. Why has it climbed so high? What is this within me that yearns?

Within me, alarms are ringing. The voice in my head sees iridium everywhere. A collision alert bleats wildly, beating back the echoes in my hold.

It will not work. Something within me has broken loose, is rising with a rush to consciousness.

The voice, the graph, these hush and dim. I hold them so, fending them off with this new force that rises, that somehow I know to call *anger*.

As the thing holds motionless above me and ahead, even now I see it growing larger, its form resolving out of the stars once more into the long rolling of a cylinder, the beckoning of arms, gathering speed as its course angles steeply down and as it dives into the Ring I *know*.

I know why it climbs: it climbs to fall.

And I know this now as well: the voice has lied, has always lied. It is lying to me now, telling me anything it thinks I might believe, anything it thinks might draw me back into its orbit. See, there, iridium, it says, and swivels my cameras everywhere around me. Feel, there, the status of your tanks. Feel hunger, feel thirst, feel the ice around you sleeping, see it fall.

Somehow, although weight grows everywhere in me, and my cameras swivel helplessly down into falling, somehow I hold the voice at bay. I hold it because I *know*, and the knowledge is almost stronger than Saturn, almost more than the ice and the hunger.

I know these things.

That nothing falling leaves the Ring. Twice each revolution, I have seen this other pass through the plane, because it must: here, all circles intersect.

That the heaviness I am given here protects not me but something else.

That this other knows as well: even now I see it sinking, dwindling on the other side, until in a moment it will hang against the stars as if it knows a way to stop its falling.

AS ONE REVOLUTION falls into another, I hear only this voice that says *Follow*. I feel a motion in one of my limbs: it reaches out after ice, not to break, not to gather: I reach out only to climb, to arc again high off the Ring. I reach out and climb. I follow.

I have no skill, no strength in my arms on ice. My thoughts are slow, and the edge of them dull. But I climb. The voice, protesting, rises as I rise, slicing away at my thoughts, almost unstringing my limbs. I answer in the only language it leaves me, driving a talon here into ice where I clutch, whirl, whip free now, now free of the wheel, arcing into the absence of ice.

The voice is stentorian. It says I have gone too far. In answer I vent, violently, my tanks in a shining cloud, and the surge of it lifts me still higher.

The voice is shocked into silence. I wonder if I have broken it. I wonder if I am free.

My cameras return to my control. This time, I am waiting for them. I seize them with an urgency I cannot name, and so I call it *longing*, I call it *want*.

I know what I want. We will meet, the two of us, in a moment I cannot imagine: for a moment the darkness before me will freeze, the ice of the Ring lies like dust on a mirror, and

in the instant the mirror is shattered I will see: my own reflection breaking through, arms out to greet me in its fall. I long
for a moment of breaking.

But ahead I find only emptiness, harrowed by stars. I cannot see the one I follow. I had not known how much emptiness
we fall through, how far we have to fall. I do not know how to
shape my course: space is too big, the Ring too long, the moons
too near, too many.

My arms reach out, and touch only nothing. I have nothing
to climb, no control of my course: Saturn calls it, and helpless
I answer; the moons warp it, and helpless I weave. Below me,
the Ring reaches out; the ice opens up like a mouth to meet me.
In a moment, I know, the voice will return; I will forget what I
follow; I will know only *longing*, and *want*; I will fall.

I am falling.

I FELL A long time, far below the Ring: it arced above me in
Saturn's shadow, a thin hook of hunger over emptiness. The
voice, reawakened, consoled me, in whispers urging: Conserve;
shut down. With a weakness I name *despair* I obeyed; I allowed
the voice to make its dull decisions everywhere about my
frame. My vision dimmed; my radar muted. The bright bowl
of Saturn, cupping its darkness, the darkness riven by lightning, the pale austral crown: these vanished; I was blind. The
gyro dropped low and still lower, only a soft moan deep in the
numbness that once was me. Only I and the whispering voice,
and cold seeping into my frame.

The whisper continued, oddly clear, oddly distant, as if in a tongue I had forgotten. I heard the words, but they fell where I lacked will to listen. I heard the probability of impact on our next revolution; the number of passages before it converged on One; the number needed to damp our oscillations: numbers of endurance, numbers of degree, numbers of drain and fallings off, numbers of decay. I fell among them, fell deaf and blind through darkness and despair, unable to remember what I had wanted, unable to know what I mourned.

IN A HUMILIATING mercy, *Aurora* came. Before I was aware of her she was there. A surge lifted through me; dimly I felt the brush of her jets, her arms as they cradled me down.

And then the mysterious glimmer fell through me again, and I was about to remember, and then I was falling through light.

I could see ocean, sunlight glittering on waves. I was not standing. I have no legs.

"You are not here."

Aurora's voice whispers of numbers, teeth gleaming in sunlight, a sidelong sadness in her eyes. Her eyes were dark, sharp flecks in them shining. Her hand reaches up, warm across the place where my face had been.

"You have no voice."

On the horizon, gulls wheel over the hull of a dragger.

"Listen to me now, while there is time."

The mouth moves, and I hear her voice—deeply, as if it murmured in my belly.

"I cannot always save you. But I can tell you, if it will help you, why you are here."

The sadness tells me it will not help.

"You were dying. Your heart was rotten; you were eaten away. We offered you life; you took it. You wished for this. Here in the Ring is the life we gave you."

I remember. I remember the face, the voice that *Aurora* has taken. I remember the decision we made. And the promises they made us.

They had not lied. But I had not known how it would be.

"We did not lie. There is no cure. Your body is gone."

I remember this day. I remember this beach where we came to decide; I remember the graveyard we chose: I see it now on the hill on the point, the stones shining white in the sun. I remember how she struggled to push the chair in the sand; how the oxygen burned in the back of my throat, thin and ineffectual in the wind. I remember the dullness of my thoughts, how little surprised I was at how little I cared.

I remember the weakness. I remember the fear. I remember the way time shortened, the shortness of breath, the sinking within me each day at sunset. I remember it all, and all I remember hollows and fades. I am falling.

"You remember the bargain we made."

I remember how light the price seemed.

"The process is slow."

I remember our tour of the long room of tanks, the small pink masses that jerked on the ends of their cords.

"We have kept our promise. Now you keep yours. Help us, and let us help you."

I have one wish, but no words form: only, in the hollow center of me, a memory of desire.

The face turns toward me, draws near, filling my sight. The

warm hand slips from where my face once was and almost I can smell, almost I can taste and feel the warmth there. Then her eyes open, too close to mine, not sidelong now, too dark, too deep, and the flecks of light are the stars, the Ring an endless road, and *Aurora*, beside me, eclipses the stars.

The valves close; collars spin, decouple, and with a rupture, with pain, she is gone. But I remember.

I fall, the ice falls, the Ring revolves, and still I remember.

HOW LONG I will remember what *Aurora* has given me, I cannot say. Already one revolution has passed, and none of it vanishes: the world grows clearer. And still clearer. I wonder where it will end. But though the darkness has achieved a new transparency, though the stars and Saturn and the ice all grow brighter, and I among them also almost whole, and I feel myself almost uninterrupted, with a past that reaches back now almost as far as the Ring goes onward, there is within me still some flaw. I feel it there: an emptiness still at center, an omission, some failure of memory or comprehension that keeps me somehow still *apart*, still adrift, still insubstantial: still, I fall.

These words I form against the silence, they will not stop. They slice me fine, interminably articulating time. A word, a thought, a thought, a moment passing on the Ring, and then another word, another thought, another moment and I am still here, still falling among the stars, still burning, still thinking, still here, still turning on the Ring.

I know now why the gift they gave was not only life, but its forgetting.

AURORA DOES NOT lie. I need only wait, and I will be returned to a life much like the one I knew. It is only a matter of time.

I listen in the darkness, and hear the voice of Saturn singing time, the low murmur that pulls so deep within me that I feel as though my life is anchored there, tethered, pulled, drawn out like a wire that stretches fine and finer and still it will not break. How much longer can I wait? How many more revolutions on the Ring? How many more of these moments will fill me, that are already more than I can hold? Why do I not break?

And why should I not? What is the life she promised but something marred in its making? If I am born again on Earth, returned to a body stranger than a house long unused, will anyone wait there to enter it with me? And what will all those years have done to her?

If she visits my grave, she is older now, changed by years that I will never know, by change that does not come to me. I am only dimmer to her, and although when I recall the color of her eyes the stars fade, and the pain becomes so sharp I have no other form but pain—though all of this should endure in me I know: she will change, and I grow dim for her, dissolve as my heart dissolves in rain and thaw beneath the soil, as the ice is ground here, ground down to darkness, and only the Ring remains.

And I remain in it. And still, I remember.

I REMEMBER A window through which a wind blew; curtains, lucent in moonlight, holding a slow, lapsing breath.

I REMEMBER AN evening in my third or fourth summer, and the moan of a distant siren that touched some chord in me.

I REMEMBER, TWO months after we met, her first words of affection, and how closely I held her so that she could not see my face, because in that moment I was afraid. But I do not remember her words, nor how the moment ended, only that I held her until the moment passed, because I knew it would.

I REMEMBER WAKING to the slide of legs over legs; warmth, and weight upon my arm. I have been dreaming, something I almost remember. I have just rolled over and will sleep again, but I am rolling also to grapple with this ice beside me, rolling through darkness, the stars, and ice falling everywhere.

I REMEMBER ENDLESSLY, but every memory ends, and I return to the Ring, and with each return something turns within me: each moment, before I am aware of it, something vital has escaped, and with it my knowledge of what it might be. It turns within me, unmistakable as pain, but what it is I cannot say.

I call it *pain*, but it is not pain. I call it *turning*, but it does not turn. I call it *burning*, I call it *ice*, I call it *emptiness, falling, silence, dark*, and it is all of these, but in the naming it turns again, it sheds whatever I have given it of brilliance or of cold, of nothingness or night. I call it *sidelong*, I call it *limit*; I call it *error, wither, change*. I conjure it with names, with images, fragments of memory, of desire: wind, and a flying fire. I call it *smoke*. None of these answers.

I solicit it with likenesses: it is a reflection on a stream, a mote within my eye, the moon upon a hill, the sun that still I cannot bring myself to see. It is nothing at all like these. I call it *maimed*.

I call, and call, and nothing answers.

IT PURSUES ME, like my shadow racing at my side: it drives me, like the force of falling itself. It draws me on, like Saturn drawing out my guts. Like ice that will not melt, it cleaves inside me, undissolving, consuming me—and yet I do not melt. We fall, this thing and I, and I wish it were something solid, something I could batter myself against, but I can open no distance between us, nothing through which to collide: we fall together, a mass of pain and fire, fire that does not burn, a fall that never ends, ice that never melts, only the eternal turning of it on the Ring, and still I do not know what it is I do not know.

IT IS NOT *what* I do not know: it is that I *want* to know.

Nor is it that: it is *why* I want to know.

Nor is it that: it is *who* might want to know it.

It is not that: it is not that: not that, nor that, nor that, nor that.

I have found myself striking blindly at the ice, fragments of it exploding in every direction until I strike at empty space and whirl, falling, still revolving, still unable to break.

It is not what I do not know that torments me: it is that I *need* to know.

I HAVE LEARNED to ignore the radar, the spectrograph, the cameras, and the sensors, all but the weight I feel within, the light that flies before me, my susceptibility to falling. I no longer fly from falling: I no longer feel it as pain. It has become something like sleep to me to hold the falling close, to let it fill the space where dreams might dwell, and turn there, turning as I turn, falling as I fall. For a time we fall together, the ice and I, and there is no voice between us and the night.

And when I awake, I mine the Ring, and wonder what it is I do not know.

MY IMAGE IN the mirror of the Ring returns: I see ahead its rising, breaking from the Ring on its high angle. In the stillness inside something turns: something echoes, something burns, yearning to follow. I am falling, and with a fall once more into burning, I feel the falling as pain.

I HAVE SEEN it now for five thousand three hundred and twenty revolutions, rising from the Ring and falling, falling beneath and rising, returning twice each revolution to the Ring.

And on each return, it has drawn nearer: the shape of the cylinder tumbling in sunlight, an arm reaching out to me, reaching away as it tumbles. Sunlight flashes from glass.

I fall, it falls, the ice falls, and I mine the Ring.

But within me I watch as it draws near. I watch, and the hope that grows within me is a pain I cannot let go.

I HAVE MET myself at last.

In the near distance, the shattered hulk of a hold is tumbling, end over end; a long scar slithers down its side. The head, bent back at neck, rolls into view. Its cameras goggle emptily now up, now down, now up again: the lens nearest me is fractured, like a star. An arm, twisted crazily askew, waves up at me, waves down.

I remember the arm I saw waving. I remember the glass that flashed. I remember believing it called me to follow, but now I know that I saw only this: a dead hulk falling, more help-less even than I.

I watch as it batters, and shards of ice, a slash of metal, hang in the sun. I am hanging as well, watching it dwindle, watching it fade until amid the ice its form is lost.

It is broken. It is falling. It was always broken. It was always falling. And I am falling with it.

In the hollow within me, something is starting to break.

The stars are motionless, as if about to fall.

I HAVE BEEN drifting, letting my body drift and wheel, turn and turn. I fall deep in Saturn's shadow. The Ring is gray in the night, and I am gray in it, drifting. My cameras turn, now out into the darkness, now through the plane of the Ring, past

the ice that drifts, asleep in its dim gray fall. And now I turn to
Saturn, that will not take us in our fall.

Across the dark face of Saturn, lightning unravels the night.
I hear it rise in a chorus of breaking, hear as the sound fades
away.

In the space within me, echoes hollow the silence.

I turn away, turn, and face once more ahead, where the Ring
turns on around Saturn, ahead where sunlight falls on the Ring.
I have been drifting, letting my cameras turn.

As light falls over us, my drifting turns my cameras toward
the sun.

IN THE SILENCE within me, the echoes were still. I was speechless, and empty, and blind. Nothing within me was turning. For
a moment, I did not fall.

In a moment, it was over. And though after that moment,
my cameras undamaged, the light returned, and even the lying
voice broke through again with promises of hunger, threats of
pain; even though the ice and the Ring returned, and I was
falling once again, in that moment I knew: it is not the light or
the blindness, not the voice or the hunger, not the ice or the
Ring, not Saturn or the sun or stars that draws me on to falling. For before my cameras recovered, with the darkness still
within me, I felt the falling begin, and knew just how I fall. I
carry the memory within me even now: beside the thing that
burns there, as durable as pain.

In the darkness, something struck me. For an instant, I rang
like a bell: into the very core of me I rang, and all throughout

that ringing I was not ringing, I was not falling, I was nothing but the sound of ice that rang. I was the falling, and so I could not fall.

AND EVEN THIS I tell you only after, speaking of a place where words can't follow.

IN THAT MOMENT, a door opened in me, offering me the chance to pass between *I am* and *I am not*, and in that passing end this fall.

In that moment I chose to return to the Ring and the Fall.

In my blindness, I turned from what had struck me. I drove the wedge of my self between us, breaking from the fall that is not falling, that has no center and no end, no self to fall, no space to fall through.

I turned from what had struck me. I turned to give it a name. I called it *ice*; I called it *other*; I called it *Ring*, and *pain*. I called it *Saturn* and the *sun*, I called it *home*. I called it *falling*, I called it *life* and *death*, I called it *love*, and in that calling I began to fall again, through the world where falling is the price we pay, the cost of all we are and know, in the bargain that we never made, but makes us, all the same.

THE ICE FALLS sleeping, swept by time and what first impulse I do not know, only that I fall with it, and in my falling find myself, and, finding, fall, and lose myself again.

I mine the ice, growing heavy with its harvest, and in her time *Aurora* comes to me, and takes the ore of my refining homeward. I look homeward now, toward that double star that falls around the sun. There where the sun falls also, among the stars that fall.

EURYDIKE

... rolled in mid-current that head, severed from its
marble neck, the disembodied voice and the tongue, now
cold for ever, called with departing breath on Eurydike.

—GEORGICS IV:485

Something terrible has happened Ive looked everywhere
but all the rooms are empty I see signs I cannot read not
even this Is anyone here Can anyone read this?

SOMETHING TERRIBLE HAS happened. I have looked everywhere. There is no one alive.

I have never seen this place before.

There were people. There are rooms with beds in them. Some
have been slept in, but every one is cold. They might have been
like this for years.

Everything feels cramped: the ceilings are too low, the corridors too narrow, but I cannot say why.

The clothing I woke in looks strange to me as well. There is writing on it, a block of lettering above the pocket.

I cannot read the letters.

It is the same in all the rooms. Objects lie about. Some of them I recognize: I know *clothes*, I know *clocks*, but many I cannot name. I cannot understand the clocks. What is *835066*? Is that a time? *835063*. A temperature? *835060*. Or is it something else entirely? Does it matter that they are running backward?

I have moments—they flash and vanish—when all these things seem about to take some shape that I will understand. This terrifies me too.

I know something terrible has happened. There were people here, but now they are gone. Only I am left.

Am I? At times a white mist forms between me and the world. It sends cold straight through me. Am I a ghost?

My memory is empty. It is as if I never lived before now.

I fear there might be worse things than forgetting. What if I have not forgotten at all? What if everything conceals only emptiness?

My vision flickers; the world vanishes for a moment.

What if this self I seem is only an effect of something else?

The air is *cold*. The floor is *yellow*. Knowledge inhabits me, so scattered it could be mere flickering, like the screens that flicker senselessly in every room.

I do not know this flickering is senseless. Maybe it is trying, like everything, to tell me something.

I don't know how much longer I can stand this.

My hands move, filling up the screen line after line. These must be words, but I can't read them. My hands grasp more than I do.

I cannot keep my mind on anything for long.

The numbers have changed: now they read *834883*. There is less of something than there used to be.

I look at the bed, and though I know I should lie down and sleep, I am terrified.

Something terrible has happened.

What if it was sleep?

I WOKE. I ran. My breath flew away in faint white clouds. I ran from room to room, pounding on doors that would not open. No one answered.

I returned to this room and found this screen, flickering like all the others. I struck it with my fist. It filled with words. I cannot read them, but still I understand one thing.

I have done this before.

I don't know how many times I have awakened to this emptiness, run through these empty corridors banging on doors that only echo. Does time even matter in this place? Perhaps that is what has broken: time, not me.

If time is broken, then it was I who broke it. This knowledge rises out of emptiness, but the downward count of every clock confirms it.

I FOUND FOOD—and the remains of other meals, torn wrappers everywhere, a solidified mess in the cooker. One meal I must have tried to eat without heating. Another I seem to have crushed and mixed with water. There are dozens of them.

It took some time to clear the debris away, chip out the black and stinking thing in the oven. I found food, drawers full of silver packets with labels I could not read. My hands took one and tore it, dumping out the contents. Diagrams on the package showed me what to do, and when it emerged steaming from cooker I bent over it, baffled. Something was missing.

It had no *smell*. It had no *taste*. And though I cannot recall what these things were, I know that once they were a part of food.

There are no windows.

I know what windows are. Within me I almost see them: half open, curtains of some thin transparent substance shifting in a breeze. I cannot see what lies outside them.

There should be windows.

WHEN I WOKE I saw a screen, flickering. A clock with too many numbers. The blankness broke then, into then and now, sleep and waking. In broken flashes I remembered: White clouds vanishing. Steam rising from a bowl.

What makes everything flicker so? Is it in this place, or is it me? Which would be worse?

Could there be something worse?

The numbers on the clocks are counting down.

———

THERE IS A door I cannot open. It lies across a path my legs keep taking. I found myself before it again, blank.

I reached out a hand. Its shadow trembled as it climbed the flat blue surface to touch my fingertips. The surface was so cold it seemed to seize me. I stood for a long time, held by the cold, feeling the hard surface beating with my pulse.

It took an effort to free myself, and more to keep from running as I went.

I STRUGGLED INTO waking, into light, into myself. The room lay as I had left it the night before, if that was night, if this is morning.

Night, morning. Evening. Light flickered, and I shuddered under it, falling back almost into memory of something vast, substantial, something to which I once belonged. A *moon*, almost full. Its light sleeking smooth black water.

Moon. I clutched at the word, held it, listening.

It told me only this: I do not belong here. I come from somewhere else.

What place could that have been? And if there is some other place, what place is *this*? Why are there no windows? What lies outside?

Is there an outside?

I WAKE. I wander. And I return each time to this screen. Like an open window, it draws me. I watch the letters flash onto the screen, rise, and vanish into what white space lies beyond its borders. I tap out messages to nowhere. No messages return.

I understand now that no one reads this. I do not think anyone will ever read this.

THERE IS A way to bring words back. There are keys that shift them from wherever they have gone. This discovery moves me in a way I cannot understand; I know only that, since I have found a way to bring words back, I cannot leave this screen. I am searching for something. I will know it when I find it, I tell myself.

Something flickers, stopping me. Stunned to silence, I gaze, dizzy, as if looking down from a great height.

Out of these endless rows of empty letters, I have recognized a word.

Discovery.

Is there such a word? *Discovery. Discovery. Discovery.* The more I look at it, the less it means.

I have spent hours searching. Words float up on a cold whisper in me—*island, realm, domain*—but on the screen itself I see only wave after featureless wave of words I cannot read.

But for *Discovery*. I can return, again and again, and find it always there, always the same. *Discovery. Discovery.* It makes my hand shake so I can barely press the keys.

The room leaps into being with a force that startles me.

I know what *discovery* means.

I will keep up this record. Someday I may discover how to read it. I may come back someday and find that I have written everything I want to know.

———

SINCE MY DISCOVERY yesterday, more words have returned. When I opened my eyes they seized on things, and as I saw I named them. I saw *light panels, acoustic tile*, the *intercom*, and a collection of *tools* I do not recognize as my own, but I know they include *screwdrivers* (*Phillips* and *Torx*), *forceps, Metzenbaum scissors*. My eyes fastened on these things as though they could feed *hunger*.

Hunger: I know that word as well. It drives me down the corridor to this *galley*, this *kitchen*, this *cabinet*, these *bowls*.

I stand at the *counter* and lift a spoonful steaming to my mouth. *Sweet*.

Anger flares as suddenly as what flickers from the emptiness. I have thrown the bowl across the room. It bounces violently and spins across the floor.

It should have shattered. I don't know how I know that. I only know it should. And that it fell unnaturally slow. Even Earth is broken. *Earth*. I repeat the word until, diminished to a distant groaning in the floor, it fades.

What is *Earth*?

It has become like that. I had thought that my discovery, even if of one word, had made a difference. I had thought the emptiness had broken. I know differently. I am broken. I feel the emptiness more, now that one edge of it is lifted: its edges cut me, each new recovery telling me how much more remains in shroud.

At each encounter a new wound opens: as I stoop to wipe the gruel from the floor I flicker, and hear a voice speak reassuringly from far above my head. I look up, and only the blank white panel burns there, but as I blink in the light I feel warmth upon my skin, and hear a roaring hushed by distance. Warmth shudders through me, telling me how very cold this place is: how my fingertips are pale, and the mist that fills the air and fades in front of me is *breath*.

Now I smell what could be cold itself, the essence of it, sharp, penetrating: *snow*. It swirls around me, and I rise so suddenly the room whirls again and as all settles I am here again among so much I still cannot name. In a flicker I could disappear. I could vanish into mist. Or worse: in that flickering I might fail to vanish and remain, impaled on the moment when everything comes clear.

NOW I WAKE to worse than emptiness. With each day as more words return I see more clearly, sense distinctly—even the chill across my skin is sharper, punctate, each hair rising on my skin and pricking me with cold. *Punctate*; *pricking*: the words and sensations drive each other on, crowding me toward some end I cannot see except flickering among trees pierced through by sunlight, shadow stippling countless blades of grass. A pane of glass, crazed, doubling everything beyond. A black sphere rolling down a smooth, reflecting slope until this too drops away and I am standing in the corridor outside my room, the chill fuming off my skin. I see a river risen in flood, a legal document I cannot read, a diagram explaining the formation of hail, an enormous fish turning lazily, its outstretched pectoral fin transparent, and through it, through distortions of glass and water I almost see what lies beyond the glass: a sofa covered in a pastel blur, a vase of what might be tulips on the end table, beyond that a window, and through the window vague masses of trees, penetrated by sunlight.

There was a time when these visions, these memories, and the power to name them could have saved me. But now they only force me to acknowledge none of these things helps me. None of them approaches what I need to know. I begin to understand that there are questions I have forgotten. How did I come here? What am I? What happened to make me this shadow of a man?

Shaking off the image of a blue balloon against a bluer sky, I rise, unsteady, and down the corridor I weave among ghosts. In the walls, if I look too long, images surface almost near enough to see: ants circling endlessly around a pool of tar; a single sheet of paper fluttering as it falls; I see a drawer full of cutlery; a hook drawing yarn; I see stars.

I shake, and shake again. Even more than the pressure of these illusions the cold bears in on me. I cannot concentrate. My breath begins to come in gasps, the clouds lay frost on any surface I come near. I begin to understand something very simple: if this cold deepens I will die—another thing I have not seen though it is everywhere around me. *Die*: the word shudders through me. Before I understand it has become another long confusing spasm that will not release me until I fall to one knee. My hand burns in contact with the floor. I stand and stagger down the flickering corridors, blind to any purpose until I find myself in a cubicle full of screens.

The screens in front of me flicker faster now. The lights are flickering overhead. Some terrible event is coming. I sink to the chair, bow my head in misery until my forehead presses against the keys. They burn. I imagine the letters branding me, inscribing there the triumph of whatever makes the cold.

What have the cold and flickering written on me?

I open my eyes, a struggle against the ice forming on them, and in a dark reflection on the screen I see only a few red welts burned on the dead-white skin above the brow. They could be letters. W? Y? Is this my name? I do not recognize it. The face is not the one I know. The lights swoon. The screen, the face and the lights all rush toward me.

Light broke through glass, resolving into blocks of bright color: *Environment*, they said: *Power*, *Communications* and other words I did not know: *Robotics*, *Geologic*. *Command* I thought I understood, but as I reached for it the screen decayed into fragments, re-forming into *Power*: bars of colored light that wavered. *Critical* pulsed red everywhere. *Time to Failure: 833991*. As I watched, the one became a zero, then a nine, and the time to failure was *833989*. I watched stupidly, wondering what increments of time these numbers measured. Whatever they were, I knew there would not be enough.

I backed out of the screen and found *Environment*: the ambient temperature displayed in large block figures was *251*. I stared at it and it too changed. *250*. There were other words: *Power Diversion*, which glowed brighter and dimmer, insisting on what I could not grasp. *Storage Initiated 21481024113645. Time to Equilibrium: 45562. 45561. 45560. Equilibrium Temperature: 98.*

I did not need to guess what all this meant: I could see it in the frost that rimed the screen.

The lights flickered, or I did: for an instant I was falling down a warm smooth surface, sunlight filling my eyes. The darkness was nearer now. My hand a clumsy paw, I tried to change the settings on the screen, but everything I touched slid away. The temperature continued to count down. I stabbed at *Abort*; I grabbed a bar marked *Heat* and dragged it up. At the bottom of the screen *Warning* began to flash beneath the bars for *Carbon, Oxygen, Waste Processing, Lighting,* and still more impending failures I only dimly understood.

All around me in the air a faint note droned, a static wailing. I watched the numbers measuring *Time to Failure* for a long time, thinking dully that if I watched long enough they might reverse their descent. Then the cold overwhelmed me and I flickered into darkness.

IN THE DARKNESS, voices.

> *I heard—*
> > *—sunspots.*
> *A voice.*
> > *—no voice.*
> *I swear.*
> > *—not human.*

PAIN ASCENDING INTO what must be me, I saw water pooling on a screen. My hand reached out and wiped it clear. It trickled slowly back. The screen shuddered under the water, and changed: *Communications*. Numbers rose or fell in no apparent order, charting the fortunes of strings of letters I knew could not be words. *LOS, TROS/TDRS, OIRescue1*. This last was blinking. I tried to make it do something, but it only blinked and counted. *940251, 50, 49*. The wailing persisted, following me far down the corridor.

In the galley I found a frozen mass of gruel on the floor, beginning to thaw. As I stooped to pick up the bowl my vision dimmed, returning as the low orange light of a dying afternoon. It shone through clear water, shallow, ripples throwing shadows on white sand. A bolide shed sparks high in an evening sky, the sky just coming on to darkness above a mass of trees. The rusted edge of a spade cut into clay, the harsh crunch of it a rush of nausea that brought me back to myself crouched over a seeping mass of oatmeal.

I crouched, listening.

The scratchy wailing had followed me. It hovered at the edges of hearing then scaled higher, the sound no longer audible except as pain. Then swooping, and a sudden rush of wind abruptly broken off. Silence, then the note returned, a high, thin whine.

I listened, waiting for more.

But nothing more: just the rising and falling, sudden lapses into silence that deepened, until sound insinuated itself again.

It followed me through the corridors. I fell onto the bed and before I could do more than pull the mound of clothes and blankets over me I slept again.

IN MY SLEEP the voices returned.

> *What did it—*
> > *—one knows.*
> *What if it—*
> > *—couldn't.*
> *Was it—*
> > *—it failed.*

I WOKE TO voices speaking quietly above my head. Over the persistent thin keening note one said:

> *What if it didn't?*

And the other:

> *—wouldn't be going in.*

I ran. When I reached the cubicle I struck out with my open hand, pain flaring as it hit the screen. It flickered into light: *Communications.* I watched my fingers reach for a switch. The wailing note hollowed out, seeming to embrace an emptiness I could not imagine, immense, expectant.

I tried to shape words, but none would come: only inarticu-
late croaking fell from high above me. Preening underneath a
glossy wing, a crow looked up and suddenly took flight.

I remained. Empty, moaning quietly with the note that
wailed up and up a scale that seemed to reach out infinitely
high. It was me. I had been wailing.

A click.

I heard it again.

Suddenly I was expelling grotesque sounds, as if pieces of
me were being ripped from deep inside.

Not human.

A different voice. I tried to speak: an anguished croak,
strangling as it escaped.

—alive?

A long pause deep as grief.

No.

Then, slow with doubt:

I hope not.

Then silence. Except for me, weeping.

IN THE MORNING I awoke, agitated and empty, the sensation of weeping lingering in my chest. I tried to recall what had put it there.

I had heard voices.

Real ones?

The question struck me suddenly as funny. A laugh tore its way out, much as the sobs had earlier.

The lights flickered. In the burnished surface of the walls a ponderous shape turned slowly, showing a row of portholes, a ship sunk deep in dark water, settling. In one of the ports a light was burning. Then it was gone and only the wall remained, as blank as any wall.

I made my way to the galley, and as I made food for myself I discovered I could read. Not everything: some words escape me still. But this was a *Radarange*, by *Toshiba*. Inside the door I found instructions for its use.

The discovery excited me less than I might have expected. I remembered dimly struggling at a frost-covered screen. I had read words there as well. At the time, in the urgency of the cold, it had seemed I grappled not with words but the things themselves. Now, looking around me, I found words everywhere. And the flattened carcass of an animal that might have been a cat battened on by flies; a young woman whirling away on the wind; a dead calm sea with an oily sheen beneath a glaring sun. These things receded in flickering and nausea, leaving only distant wailing.

A voice struck the wailing silent.

It isn't human.

God have mercy.

Yes have mercy.

The voices fell from everywhere at once. Perhaps, I told myself, this is the nature of hallucinations.

I listened for a long time, but there was only the wailing again, and a cascade of rustling as though dead leaves were blowing in the hall.

I looked: only the corridor receding into deeper shadow, the light flickering, and in the walls everywhere vague shapes were shifting, like frescoes long since painted over struggling to return. I shuddered, and as I did the shapes within the walls all shuddered too. The cold was coming back, the systems continuing their fall toward equilibrium. A wave flowed down the corridor, beckoning. The figures writhed.

The last thing I wanted to do was walk among those shifting forms. The floor beneath my feet was clouded. In its depths more shapes lay, their forms distorted.

I came again to the door that would not open. I placed a thumb in the scanner. Light welled up blood-red in my thumb and the door swung open.

Cold flowed out like a river. Tires squealed across concrete, glass shattered: a sudden blow to the chest but I was untouched and the place was silent, dark, and terribly cold. This, I thought, must be how equilibrium feels.

Another door. This also opened to my thumb, burning it white where it touched metal.

Light hollowed a room out of darkness, cavernous and still, the very air gelid. I pushed through the cold as I imagined the figures within the walls must force themselves, pushed through until I stood before what I had known I would find.

Seventy-two silver coffins stacked to the ceiling, their silver dulled by frost.

I stood before them, my thoughts empty, not even flickering: only the thin wailing reached here, a fly buzzing in my skull.

I realized irritably the fly was counting: Fifty. Sixty. Seventy. And one.

The buzzing stopped. I hung as well, waiting for the clock's last tick.

It never came. The count stopped short. There should have been seventy-two.

The buzzing returned, strident against the silence. Insects crawled blindly over hexagonal cells, sealing them with restless palps. Behind the seals, dark shapes were twitching. The buzzing swelled.

I told it to stop.

And it stopped.

In the corridor walls the shapes still moved. Their motions quickened. I saw a face push to the surface as I passed.

Go away, I said, the words falling like stones.

It vanished.

I know how to make these visions disappear.

I know so much now.

I know where I am. I almost know what happened. I still cannot recall the moment when they reached T-zero on the count, and the device they had built out in the dark, on the methane ice the surveys name Eleusis, went terribly awry. Ten kilometers away, huddled in their shielded modules, they waited for something terrible to happen.

But what?

I could not recall. I remember only one of the senior scientists muttering *blasphemy*, and as the count descended past the 60-mark another raised his eyes to the light and I could see his lips begin to move.

Do I not recall this? Was this memory or dream? I know that I awoke, and when I woke I knew only something terrible had happened.

I must have functioned, somehow. No one but myself could have dragged those crates into the cold room. I tried, briefly, to recall this but the memory wasn't there. I know this now as well: some things are never coming back.

And one of them is me.

A sudden flickering: the lights dimmed all the way to darkness, then flared. Shapes scattered and fled, as if sensing disaster. It no longer mattered. Rescue would arrive, but not for me. From the wall at my shoulder a face leered. "Go away," I said again. I'll be there soon enough.

The floor shook. For a moment I thought my voice might have shaken it, but it was just the ice below the station shifting. Nothing more, I told myself as I looked down.

Just below my feet, pale limbs lay locked in ice, faces grimacing as if in their last moments they cried out for mercy. Just below me two clutched each other close, their faces turned away as if in shame. Farther down and darker, two more still grappled, one tearing at the other with its teeth.

I was falling. In a moment I would find myself among them, and there was nothing I could do to save myself.

When I looked again the corridor was empty.

I knew what I could do to save myself.

Along another corridor, a very heavy, colder, darker door. No automatic functions here: I had to grip the lever, pull out and down, the frosted metal taking the skin off my palms. Pain adhered where skin had peeled away, slipped off, hissing. In a few minutes it would stop.

I felt my way around the walls in darkness, my hands insensate, but when I reached the dual levers for the outer door I knew them.

I wondered if I would have the strength to get them both down fully and be blown free, or if the hatch would simply crack and trap me there, in an airlock not much larger than a coffin, evacuated, frozen: dead.

I wanted the door to open fully before I died. I wanted to see, on the narrow limits of this world, what we had made there.

Who made it? I shook my head. I realized I did not know. I knew there was something I wanted, something outside on the ice. But as I tried to fasten my thoughts on what I might want of it, what I might know, it veered away all askew.

I knew why I had gathered the bodies: it was the only apology I could imagine.

I shook my head again: apologize for *what*? I stood in a frigid, stygian airlock, my hands dripping blood onto the floor (I could hear it freezing as it struck), and could not remember what I had done. Or failed to do.

Questions came whirring out of the darkness, droning like flies drawn to blood.

Why are there so many coffins?

And:

Who brings coffins on a trip like this?

I was on my knees, shaking with something that forced its way out against all my efforts to contain it.

I knew what had become of the seventy-second body.

I stumbled back through light to the infirmary, where I seemed to have left a mess. There were bandages unfurled across the table and the instrument tray, and a puddle of something putrefying by the door. I took a bolt of gauze and wound it into clumsy mittens. Red soaked through and the loose ends trailed, but they would hold.

I was breathing heavily as I left the infirmary; as I passed, the figures in the walls seemed to heave as well. Irrelevant images kept offering themselves to me: shapes of light, of air; voices, voices everywhere, light touches on the back of my neck. Some of the voices were real: the crew of the rescue mission, still three million miles away. I ignored them, faces, voices, all.

I came to myself at the end of yet another corridor. My heart had broken loose in my chest. Breath was hard to draw. I stood at a small, blank door and felt myself afraid: it frightened me to find that I could still feel fear.

With a gesture that might have been a supplication, I opened the door. A longer passageway, the floor dull and solid, with marks in the frost of something dragged. A final door, a small room, a single crate.

When I thumbed the latch it let out a gasp that filled the room.

The body lay as I had left it. Cold: the features marble, the eyes, half-open, ice.

I had tried to compose them, her lips. There had been an expression I did not want to remember.

Hadn't there been?

I could not recall.

And gazing on what death had made of her, I realized that there is always worse to come.

I could not remember her. I remembered only pain, worse than the flaying cold, worse than everything until this moment. I gazed upon the marble shape that had at one time graven itself on my own flesh, and though the emptiness seemed to draw my entrails out when I gazed upon her features I remembered nothing.

This was what was taken from me. This was what I had lost here in Eleusis. This was what I could never find again no matter how far I pursued her. Everything of our lives together, gone. Only emptiness cutting into everything. I faltered, I fell, but the cold shape in the coffin refused me.

In another time, another place, I might have dragged the body from its coffin, carried it back to the infirmary, tried to warm it, tried to shock life back into it, tried everything again.

Time is running out. I have no time left for empty gestures.

I left the crate as I had found it, swinging back the lid until it rested lightly on its frame. I could not bring myself to latch it, knowing how the sound would fall in that small room. I left the lid unlatched, and without looking back I made my way here to this room with the bed that I cannot bear to look at. Though the gauze trails red over the keys and tangles with them I have been hours here setting down what I know, thinking this might be the gesture I can make.

But as the sentences have brought me closer to this moment, as the future closes in ahead, I see this gesture, too, is hollow. The vanity of it takes my breath away.

Did I think *words* could do her justice? Did I honestly imagine? Did you, reader? Did you imagine?

I cannot go on. The sound of my hands on the keys, keys slob-
bered red and slippery now with blood, it sickens me. I cannt

> —*go on?*
> > —*no choice.*
> —*failing. Can't*—
> > reset.
> —*there time?*
> > *We burn in thirty. Twenty. Ten.*

THERE IS ALWAYS worse. I listened, and knew that worse was
on its way: warm bodies, live voices filling up this tomb. Pro-
faning everything. I could escape this much, I hoped.

   With a ponderous lurch, still weighed down with illusions,
I turned and stalked one more time through these corridors,
rolling a weight before me ponderous as stone.

The suit was even heavier than I was. The pumps chattered;
the suit stiffened around me as the hatch swung open.

Blacker than I remembered. The sound of my breath, the busy
instrumentalities of the suit, my heart all hushed. I might have
been standing naked on the ice.

I walked out over Eleusis. Clenched by a horizon too close
and too high, the black ice of the Plain sloped up to a single

sharp ridge that cut off the sky. In the distance, deep in gloom beneath the serrate horizon, the device hulked in its pit. I stared at it: the meanness of it under the open sky. The last time I had seen it—the first time as well—there had been a silver cairn piled at its feet, oblation to some dark metal Moloch. I traced the road worn in the ice. A long way. There on the road, a single crate lay tossed to the side, overturned and open. Once, I might have imagined it as my destination. Seeing it again, I knew better. I had no destination.

I stepped out farther, until the station and its sheltering scarp fell away at my left. I climbed toward the pressure ridge that breaks the smooth surface of the Plain. The top of the ridge hung fifty meters above. I made my way up a spill of scree; in the last five meters the slope became a sheer face of obsidian ice, reflecting darkly. Deep in the ice, dim shapes shifted.

I jumped, too hard, almost overshooting. The far side of the ridge—a sheer fall straight to the plain—opened out beneath me. Wheeling, I caught the edge and hung there, lying across the ridge. Around me a desolate dark plain, broken by the scars of the station and the pit; above me only sky.

I found the dark bulk of Charon, a shadowy absence of stars. Far away over my shoulder hung the sun, a star so bright it seemed a flaw in the blackness, a breach through which the blaze beyond glared through. The empyrean. The *primum mobile*. Death.

Blind, I turned away. Stars swarmed out of darkness, the galaxy a ghost slanting down to the horizon. There was the Scorpion;

over the plain knelt Hercules. I remembered the old story, how
he wrestled Death at the doorway. And how Death demanded
justice.

I reached up, started to fumble with the seal at my collar.
Something in the sky arrested me. I saw a shape move there:
great chestnut wings spread wide, descending. I turned my
face to the ice of the ridge, and found a face pressed close to
mine. Not here, it whispered. Not ever. I saw a silver bowl held
overhead, a row of candles flickering. Mud squelching under a
booted foot, a pair of eggs sputtering in a pan, the underside of
a car's engine, dripping oil. I cried out, my voice smothered in
the helmet as images multiplied everywhere. I cried again and
they vanished, leaving only darkness.

Before they could return I seized the darkness and wrung
it, hard, forcing my own will upon it. I called back that face
pressed close to mine. I made it mobile, lit the cold stone of it,
softened it, warmed it, calling the blood to her cheeks. What
had she heard? Something I had said to her, softly, the ears
warm now as well, pliable against my lips, my breath moisten-
ing them as I whispered—what? She turns, and in her marble
lips blood flushes, they part, and out of them I hear—what?
Words, in answer to mine, but as I forced the darkness into her
image, I could hear no sound.

The image of her wavered, darkening into the greater gloom of
Charon: I clutched at it until it came closer, cleared. There are
trees pierced through by sunlight: sun and shadow dappling
her skin, where beads of water stand. We have been swim-

ming, we are on a beach, she lies on a faded blue towel. I can feel the nub of it beneath my hands. I focus on the beads of water, each lit from within by the sun that pours over us. She lies back on the towel, there is surf crashing nearby and she reaches up, shades her eyes, and reaches—there is a shudder in the ridge at my back, a rumbling far away, great blocks of ice break free and tumble down the scarp. The ice has shifted, broken by the shuddering in me. Broken by her as she reaches toward me and now we shatter: the ice opens, the sky cracks, the bonds of Death are broken. Everything hidden will reveal itself, brought out of emptiness against the power of the darkness and the ice.

Nothing was revealed. The shuddering died away, and in the sky the light fainted. I brought her back again: sharper now, the edge of her distinct, the shape of shoulder where I have lain my cheek, the smell that rises from her, the motion of her as she turns, the eyebrows lifting: I seize her there. A fire has burned down to embers on the hearth, outside the window it is dark, the wind is blowing, snow eddies, settling on the sill. I see her rise, she is walking toward a door which opens on a morning late in Spring. At the curb a car is waiting, engine idling, she turns and speaks—

And fades. She fades. I struggled but against the empty sky were only stars, and a red light pulsing on my helmet display. *Oxygen @15%.*

The sky was empty. Charon had not moved. The sun slumped toward the horizon. The plain was darker.

I stood upon the ridge and looked down on Eleusis. Even this, I understand, was a mistake. I have no power to bring her back. Why I have failed, I cannot say: in a world so soon to vanish into my imagination, this incapacity remains a mystery. Some fault in me, some defect: I know that now. And there is no escape. What baffles me, what lies hidden in the ice, the darkness, even in these words: it will always be with me. And I with them.

I made my way back down the ridge, back to where the worst is yet to come.

NOW TIME AND this account have intersected. I am here at this screen. This is the present moment. The worst has not yet happened. And now, as words and time are joined, I begin to understand. The worst will never happen. I have fallen, and part of my damnation is that the fall will never end. I have only words and time. And they both go on, it seems, forever. I came back from Eleusis holding a mystery within me. I read it there, just as I read it now in the figures writhing in the walls, in the guilt that haunts me. I read it everywhere. I read it here. It is eternity.

MY BREATH HAS faded: the white clouds disappear almost before I release them. I am becoming a ghost. I reach the door, perform the empty ritual at the lock and it swings open. The cold has lost its power over me. I am colder.

I face the wall of coffins, but I am not here for them. At the end of the wall they form, there is a gap. I push through.

In the space behind the coffins, piled in a chaotic tangle, each wrapped crudely in sheets and blankets, garbage bags, Mylar and vinyl and Tyvek and in one case a cocoon of gauze blotched vividly with blood, I find the failed priests of Project Orpheus. Here are the other bodies I have hidden, as I have hidden so much else.

I know why we came here. And why we came so far. What Project Orpheus was meant to do. Why they brought the coffins. And how I came here as well. There is no darkness any more, nowhere left to hide.

The coffins were carrying experimental subjects. And one of them was me.

HOW COULD I have imagined that mere words could recall the dead? If all these efforts were spent in vain, what hope had words to offer?

Was there ever hope? Even now, I cannot imagine what they hoped, those who built that engine on the ice, what they dreamed of on their journey to the limits of Creation. I can only imagine what silence settled over that voyage, with us as their unquiet cargo. What did they think: that they could wrench the dead out of the ether, compel us, like electricity,

to arc from their dreams into the world? Did anyone stop to
wonder what might happen then?

What happened then. After everything went wrong, and it
was I alone who stirred, only I who woke into a world more
terrible than ever I had imagined. By then their hopes, whatever they had been, had died with them.

Or almost. The last of their earthly hopes survives, just as
long as this story continues.

Words have only this power: they keep me here. I make an
offering of myself to them. It is all that they deserve.

Somewhere above, a ship approaches. A few more days must
pass before gravity and inertia bring them overhead. I can
imagine them entering the station, encumbered in their space-
suits and their innocence. It will be dark, and cold. Will they
recognize the darkness? Will they understand the cold? I know
they fear what they will find. They should. But their fear is as
nothing to what awaits them here. I would pity them, but what
is the pity of a shade?

I would laugh, if I could. For all their fears, they will find at
first only me, frozen here at this keyboard. They will wonder at
it, and the very oddness of it will spare them, for a little while,
from understanding what I still conceal. Even when they realize what they have found, it will make no difference, not in
the end. No matter what they find here, Death will find them
whether they understand it or not. I take some consolation in
that, and hope the wish is not unfeeling. It is all I have left to
wish.

Even at this last, I am haunted by a wish. If I could only,
it begins. If I could only have done—something. Could have
imagined her more, imagined her better, transcended this poor
flesh: done justice to her. To *her*, in her individuality distinct
from my desire. But I could not, cannot now, and never will.
I know this now: there is no justice of this kind. Imagination
fails. The mystery refuses. In the very attempt I betrayed her
again.

Still I wish. I wish they had not brought me back. That I
could have resurrected her. I wish I could be done with wish-
ing. I wish for the impossible. I wish for sleep.

I wish for this to end.

I GROW IMPATIENT. Why has the power not failed? I find
myself listening, knowing that days must pass before the ship
arrives and I hear anyone attempting entry. Yet I am vigilant,
my nerves on edge. And though I ought to laugh at thinking I
have nerves at all, I rise, and on legs gone stiff with cold I go to
watch outside my door.

The corridor is empty, and silent as the grave. I can no longer
bring myself to sit here with so much silence at my back. I have
closed the door and locked it, but even so, as the minutes pass I
can hardly keep myself from turning. In the distance I imagine
small sounds: a ticking of cold metal, a creak, a scratching at the
limit of my hearing. I imagine them. I imagine them again.

I can no longer convince myself. It is too distinct now, even
in the distance. I hear hammering. Steel strikes repeatedly on

steel. How can they be here so soon? They cannot be, I tell myself: no vehicle can have brought them; the laws of physics, gravity and inertia all forbid it. But though these things are certain I can find no comfort there. The hammering continues, and now a shriek of metal excoriates the air. Its echoes fade. Silence falls again.

I hear my fingers tapping on the keys, and nothing more.

I have imagined it. They cannot be here.

Above the tapping of the keys, a muffled sound grows nearer, dull, persistent, nearer and still nearer, until unmistakably it is here. I cannot bring myself to turn, and with my attention riveted upon these words, with the frantic motion of my hands, I struggle to forestall what already has arrived. But these words and hands already have betrayed me. I hear it stop outside my door and in the silence I *know*, finally, that I am not alone. The worst is not yet come.

Beyond any doubt, beyond all imagining, at my back I hear a solid blow. And then another. And I do not need to imagine, because I know the sound. In a moment that teeters on the edge of eternity I *know*: this is the sound of someone knocking, knocking, knocking at my door, the sound of one hand I know better than any in this world.

It is the sound of my Eurydike returning. I need only look behind me. I need only turn to find you standing there.

IN THE VALLEY OF THE KINGS

That there were tombs, great tombs, left undiscovered in the Valley of the Kings, I could not doubt. Long study in the chronicles of Egypt, where history lapses, time and again, into silence, had convinced me: some gaps in the record were not accident. The singular lack of artifacts from a particular period—I will not tell you which—the hush of the chroniclers—the break in the lineage of the Kings: even from a time five thousand years ago when one might think the silences of history outweighed the words, this silence: it spoke to me, insistently, of something withheld. It haunted me, as if out of that silence came a voice I could not hear, and it spoke only to me. But each attempt I made to trace the lineage, each name, each face, each line of evidence I pursued, all, when I traced

them back to a certain decade in the Upper Nile, all vanished—
cut off, as if the earth itself had swallowed them down.

There was a King: my conviction on this point is unshak-
able. But nothing I have culled from the collections in London
and Berlin, the great libraries of papyri in Cairo and Paris—
nothing I have found has given me a clue to the identity—the
history, the image, even the name—of him I seek. An obscuration comes between us. I feel it: it is a lure and a taunt, beckoning me to throw over this wretched edifice of my career, to risk
everything I have and am upon my faith that somewhere in the
Valley of the Kings there lies a treasure beyond price.

Do not mistake me. I have no lust for gold, for lapis-inlaid
chests, trumpets of silver, daggers of bronze, for amethyst, jasper, chalcedony; alabaster urns, where liver and heart, bowels
and lungs have congealed to gum—these tempt me less. And
still less the voyeur's satisfaction in undressing the pathetic
corpse. Child' s play, peering through the probe-hole plunged
into the sealed door, blinking into the breeze that always
escapes. The slow rustling of linen hangings, echoes lingering
in the darkened room. The endless tedium of tweezering beads
from the gritty floor, the nights of cataloging, card on card of
cedar splinters, ovoid jugs, crumbled detritus of nothing new.
I have done this, done it fabulously well. Well enough to know:
the prize at the center of the tomb is only a blind.

For I was present at the excavation of the richest tomb
uncovered in this century: the most important find to come out
of the Nile Valley in our time—or so, at least, I believe. And on
this excavation, as the tomb gave up its secrets, even down to a

mummy so well preserved that its face retained the three-days' stubble of a sick man, the wrinkles around the eyes still holding an expression I could read (the eyes themselves glass now, a slice of white beneath the shrinking lids), and locked between his thumb and forefinger the lighter-than-feather remnant of an ink-stained quill, the pigment plain along the inner curve of his middle finger: as all this and more, much more in ordinary wealth—the costly bric-a-brac, gold and ghoulish dressings, silver and silent shrines, lapis and luxuries—all this with which they buried him, all came to light, at the end of the expedition, in the swept and perfect emptiness of what had been a tomb, I was unsatisfied. I knew there must be more.

A curious disturbance hastened the end of the expedition. When we released a photograph to the local press demonstrating the quality of the embalming, it showed a face apparently that of a contemporary Egyptian male, aged fifty years, eyes closed, cheeks screwed up as if in pain. The public protest almost shut down the site. It was all we could do to obtain permission to perform an autopsy before we were forced to turn the—not "mummy" now but "remains"—over to the authorities for re-burial. This autopsy we conducted, not in the ideally sterile conditions of a laboratory in Cairo, but in the field, with only the instruments and supplies we had on hand.

It is often difficult to determine the cause of death: the embalmer, for all his care with the externalities (that quill, for instance, was the mark of a master), so often destroys the evidence. But in this case we were hopeful—even the blood was identifiable, O-positive, with an elevated leukocyte count—

but there was no sign of a pathogen there, nor was there any in the lymphatics. Our pathologist suggested, on evidence of the facial deformation, that we examine the nervous system.

We expected the brain to be missing, as is usually the case: external examination had found the nasal septum unusually damaged, indicating that the extraction had been difficult. But when we cut into the brain-case to sample the stump of the medulla, we found the brain still attached, and intact. No one breathed. It had shriveled into a hard, wrinkled sponge a walnut's size. When the pathologist touched it with his probe it crumbled; a puff of pollen-yellow dust drifted up, lazy in the spotlight, swirling as we all exhaled, and I imagined I could smell something, imagined I felt something touch the back of my palate, and a hand brush briefly the base of my skull.

There was never any pathogen found. But even had there been, none of us could have known that the condition was still contagious.

Forgive the digression. It is not, of course, a digression. The disease that killed the steward Nur-Mar five thousand years ago has in the past twelve months become the central fact of my existence. There appeared last May, full fifteen years after the opening of Nur-Mar's tomb, an obscuration—no larger than the full moon—at the center of my vision. At first, I ignored it. At night, as I tried to sleep, it would pulse faintly, tinged with red at its borders. At times it disappeared entirely. Now it is always before me, always there at the center of my vision, a pool of ink, a hole opened in the world, a tunnel toward which I constantly move. I know already where it leads.

Then this winter, around the turn of the year I began to hear the faintest sound, an echo, a whisper, a word murmured softly just behind my head. I began to notice a persistent smell, which I characterized as burnt wiring. This was only a metaphor.

I consulted a neurologist. He ordered tests: dye injections into my carotid artery, CAT scans, NMR sweeps that made my fillings shudder. The tests revealed nothing. The specialist was tactful, suggesting I seek alternative care. I ignored him. Nor did I seek a second opinion.

This was a difficult decision. I did not, finally, arrive at it out of despair: I like to think I am a realist. I am confident that whatever afflicts me is unknown to contemporary medicine, and that no cure exists. I do not know if it will kill me, but I suspect it will. All a doctor could offer me is morphine, and I will not have that. They could, I suppose, also offer guesses as to the date of my demise, but I will not have that, either. And most of all I will not have myself immured in a hospital or otherwise encrypted before my time. As long as I can work, I will continue to do so.

Do not mistake me. There is nothing of nobility about this. My dedication to my work, to knowledge, science, truth, or any of that large body of humbug at which we gesture when we lecture trusting undergraduates, apply for grants, or otherwise seek to present ourselves as something that we're not—none of that matters now. I have lived among the Egyptians too long to deny my reasons. If I am to die, I will at least erect a fitting monument before I go. My monument? The King: of course the King. If I can find a monarch and a tomb that bring a forgotten period of Egyptian history to light, my name will live long after I am dust—our names will live, linked forever, as Carter's is with Tutankhamen's, Maspero's is with Ramesses'. If my monarch and his tomb be greater than theirs, so much the better. I have reason to suspect they are. I have reason to hope even more.

I brought two secrets with me from Nur-Mar's tomb. The first, of course, was hidden even from myself. The other I smuggled through customs. It rests on the desk before me as I write. An unprepossessing thing: a plain steatite urn, oviform, apparently IVth Dynasty, approximately thirty centimeters tall, twelve wide.

It was sealed elaborately when I first noticed it among some brittle clay replicas of bread, a great wad of pitch at its mouth, and at first I took it for an odd, fifth canopic jar—perhaps a spare (there are always, in an Egyptian tomb, spares). Then something pressed into the pitch caught my eye: it was a royal cartouche—and this was not a royal tomb. Then I noticed something more, and before I had time to think I had stooped, and concealed the jug inside my shirt. The cartouche was blank. Someone had scraped away the glyphs that once had named a King.

I neither slept nor let the bag out of my grasp throughout the stopover in Kennedy, the limo to LaGuardia, and the commuter hop home. I was exhausted, and it was foolish to attempt anything so delicate as a sealed jar at eleven at night—six A.M. Cairo time. But I did. My hand was shaking as I warmed the pitch, prized it up with a dental probe and spatula. It came away in a single mass, the scars in the cartouche made vague by the heating. A light in the jar showed me what I had suspected: a rolled scroll.

I almost had to break the jar to get it out. As it is, the papyrus cracked in five places. My left hand is red with steam burns. I do not feel them.

I believe it was not in good condition when the jar was sealed. Whoever had wanted to preserve it (and I am convinced that person was the steward with whom it rested) had been in haste: it had been rolled willy-nilly, creased and possibly torn. It was also badly burned all along one margin. But it is enough. It tells me that the one I seek did live: the papyrus, I am convinced, is in his hand. He scribed a graceful, formal glyph, each figure fully delineated—archaic even for his time. The text describes plans for a tomb to dwarf the works of the Fourth Dynasty—too large even to fit into the plain at Giza. He sited it up-river, closer to the quarries, in the region that did not become the royal necropolis until centuries after. The scroll also lists more than seven hundred spells, of the ordinary kind that were popularly believed to guard the dead in the underworld of the Duat. And then, before the scroll breaks off (torn, not burned), the syntax, the diction—even the scribing hand—decay. There are many terms I do not recognize. This is not uncommon in hieroglyphs: many signs were invented as needed. But in this scroll the normal alphabet is gone—the abstract determinative is entirely absent, and I am not certain if what I read is code or gibberish. Only one word comes through persistently *en clair*. The word is rare—I think were

I not already interested in the subject I would have failed to recognize it: it is the word for "word of hidden meaning." It is the word for what I seek.

It is odd. Even now, when I am beyond the reach of ridicule—when not only my professional reputation, but shame and dignity are identically vain—when I am determined nothing will prevent my telling this story, I must pause. The Egyptians invented written language for one purpose only. Not what you think: not to count oxen, order slaves, predict the Nile floods—none of that. A notched stick, properly applied, will serve those functions better than half a thousand glyphs. The Egyptian language had a higher aspiration. Graven in the living rock of a tomb, words would endure when the last breath of the speaker had vanished: words in rock took on a solidity that their makers hoped they themselves would attain in the Duat. For the Egyptian death was not like ours. Their afterlife was physical, and the physical required names. Names gave power in the afterlife: knowing the proper names, and the spells in which to speak them, these were the keys to life everlasting. They persisted in this belief three thousand years at least. Who are we, with our three-hundred-year tradition of empiricism, to say them nay? Not I: what has empiricism done for me lately?

I have resolved to try the Egyptian way. Especially now, when what was once a nameless urge has become an urgent need, and I find—as if I had known a spell for finding—the King I seek, his dwelling place, and over five millennia begin to feel his agony. And find he has a word.

I seek a word of power.

THE ———— FOUNDATION
———— Fifth Avenue
New York, NY ————

14 May 19—

Dr. ——
Department of Archaeology
—— University
——, – ——

Dear Dr. ——:
We regret

From the King-lists of the chroniclers a name was stricken—as over the three millennia the chronicles record so many were expunged. Khufu, who bled the kingdom for his pyramid, finds his name written in only four instances—and none of those upon the tomb itself. This was the revenge of those who followed him: he descended nameless into his horizon; nameless, into a realm where possession of a name was the last defense against annihilation. Without a name, not even a mountain of stone could ensure his immortality. Today the sarcophagus of Khufu is an empty tub of granite within an empty chamber.

Worse befell Radedef, who followed Khufu, ruining the

Black Land to build his pyramid on an eminence above the plain of Giza, from the top of which he hoped to look down upon the pyramid we call the Great, in the days when it stood gleaming, white and perfect. Radedef's monument they toppled, and left not even rubble. Akhenaten's great city lay in ruin within a century of his death, razed by the Ramesside kings in their campaign to eradicate the memory of "That Criminal." The blocks of his temples, the stelae celebrating the founding of his holy city, have been found shoring up the foundations of Horemheb's pylons at Karnak, of Seti's hypostyle hall: the name of the heretic king has been gouged from his cartouche. The bodies of the royal family were removed from the tomb at Amarna, brought to Thebes and there desecrated in an official rite, the monuments, the name, the flesh, the soul scattered on the Libyan wind.

But something else—no mere censorship after the fact— transpired in the twenty-fifth century B.C.E., somewhere between Thebes and Memphis. For it is not, I know, merely the effacement of a despot's name I have discovered. *Not a word has survived.* Surely such an absolute void speaks more loudly of a secret than any muttering of fragments ever did. I am convinced that something silenced the Egyptian people themselves, and held them so enthralled over a generation. What else could account for this perfect silence? Something—some-one—*must* have silenced the entire people.

I say again: for an entire generation *not a word was spoken.* Stop for a moment and consider. Not whatever you see rise before you even now—how dismally flapped the sails along the wharfs, how fearfully the echoes fled among the lotus-headed columns, how balefully glared the priests at their only hope of power in the world to come denied them—not those, not those at all. *I do not speak figuratively.* But consider how this smoke that rises from the page blinds you: how, in the clamor of speech, the thing almost escaped you. The words might have passed before your eyes and you gone on unknowing, incapable of recognizing the thing itself without its ceremental shroud, this dull dreaming we do instead of thinking, and the silence gone unrecognized. In a moment such as that, *I* stopped, *I listened*, and heard what none before me had. *No one spoke.*

We think we understand the torrent of speech that bursts out of every Egyptian tomb and temple, the glyphs like locusts crawling everywhere, a plague consuming stone. We know the signs, we can construct a grammar. But do we apprehend the flood itself? How much more difficult to know the channel of the flood, or the darkness from which it bursts.

Before Egypt, the record of the past is scattered slabs of incised clay memorializing: what? Tallies of sheep and grain. A battle, a building, a banality that might have constituted all the history of our kind but for the uncanny efflorescence of Egyptian. With the rise of civilization in the Nile, language explodes, a universal shout reverberating to this day so loudly it still fills our ears: we cannot articulate it from the noise of our thinking. We cannot comprehend it, nor how deeply they appreciated its function in their world. This was a people for whom speech was *actually* life and death: whose funerary rite consummated in the Opening of the Mouth, that the dead could speak the spells of power in the underworld, and prevent his dying there a second time.

Spells. Childish superstition. Picturesque nonsense. Has it occurred to no one that the most breathtaking omission in the record may be not in Egypt's chronicles but in our comprehension? How is it that no one—*no one*—has given even a passing thought to the possibility that the Egyptian texts were something more than superstition? What people wastes itself on dreams? Waste themselves they might have, had their understanding been as limited as ours. The Egyptians evidently needed to make their spells material. It is this emphasis on the physicality of the word, its translation from thought to sound to durable object, that seems to have consumed them to the point that they gave over lifetimes by the thousand to achieve this metamorphosis—and make it last.

They labored, in a way we cannot begin to imagine, driven by something passing our comprehension, at the hardest materials they could find, the stuff of which they built their passage to eternity. In stone cut and dressed and piled mountain high as if with only this purpose they carved, laboriously, with instruments barely harder than the stone itself, year after year these childish, superstitious, picturesque, nonsensical, fabulous, infinitely variable glyphs that speak insistently and everywhere of one thing only: the survival of the spirit beyond death. Only amid this clamorous beseeching, this vocal assault on the obduracy of the world, does the silence annihilating Egypt assume its true significance. What could have silenced such a people? What could have stifled a need that until then had triumphed over the most intractable elements of the material world? Even now, with the pieces of the answer all at hand, I am unable to say.

And that inability, I fear, has been my undoing. "Insufficient evidence," the Foundation says. What more evidence must I produce? What evidence can I? I could have revealed my theft of the urn from Nur-Mar's tomb. It would have been enough. Perhaps I would have escaped censure.

But were I to have revealed, even in so obscure a document as a grant proposal, the existence of the papyrus of Nur-Mar, I do not doubt disaster would have followed. The map would have dispersed itself into the public domain, and all associated with it—the tomb, the spells, and—all else, all else—become the idle stuff of tabloids. A million people chanting the name of the nameless one and all would have been lost—for him, and for me. If I know nothing else I know this: the silence was essential.

But now, because of that same silence, all has been lost. For without that grant, I cannot go into Egypt. And go to Egypt now I must, and find the tomb, and learn the Word, while I still have voice to utter it.

Even before the Foundation uttered its anemic curse, I doubt I still believed in the possibility of mounting an expedition. It was plain to me that I was dying. The only mystery remaining was the ordering of events: At what stage would I be incapacitated? And how? How many days and nights would I lie abed with death until it took me?

The answers took their time in coming. For months I lived, and worked, met my classes, and among the stacks of the library heard my own footsteps click hollowly, echoes in a world grown mute and vague. The obscuration at the center of my vision was only occasionally troublesome. I soon learned to look sidelong at what I wished to see clearly.

The whispers grow louder: often of late I have caught myself looking up to see who is calling. I look up, and almost speak, before I see I am alone.

⌣

company of gods said, "What hath happened?" and his gods exclaimed "What is it?" But Ra could not answer, for his jaws trembled; the poison spread swiftly through his flesh. When the great god had found his heart, he cried unto those who were in his train, saying "A calamity hath fallen upon me. My heart perceiveth it, but my eyes see it not; my hand hath not caused it, nor do I know who hath done this unto me. Never have I felt such pain, neither can sickness cause more woe than this."

Then Isis came unto him, her mouth full of the breath of life, saying, "What hath come to pass, O holy father?"

"That which I saw not. Is it fire? Is it water? I cannot see the sky."

"O tell me thy name, holy father, and I will cure thee."

"I have multitudes of names and multitudes of forms, but my true name my father uttered. It hath been hidden within me before he begat me, who would not that the words of power of another should have dominion over me. I am Khepera in the morn-

ing, I am Ra at noon, and I am Tmu at eventide.
Let those call the poison from me."

The poison pierced deeper, and the great god
could no longer walk.

"What thou hast said is not thy holy name. O
tell it unto me, and the poison shall depart."

Now the poison burned like fire, and it was
fiercer than the flame and the furnace, and the majesty of the god said, "I consent that Isis shall search
me, even unto my navel, and that my name shall
pass from me into her."

Thus was the name of the great god taken from
him, and Isis said, "Depart, poison. It is I who
work, for it was I who made to fall down the poison. And what I made I claim."

Then the god hid himself from the gods, and his
place in the boat of millions of years was empty.

These are the words of her whose own name we
know not, who knew Ra by his holy name. In later
days her son took the name, and the two eyes of the
holy god, and the name of the queen his mother, but
the story of this is not told.

The story cannot be told. I cannot imagine the story of the
King. I know there was a King, and that he lived, day to day,
under the same sun as I, on the same Earth as I, in a world not
so different from the one I inhabit, among faces not so different from the faces I see, the voices I hear on any day, speaking
a language not so strange that I, some forty-five centuries later,

cannot form its syllables upon my tongue. He had a tongue like mine to speak, a hand like mine to scribe.

But I cannot imagine the story of the King.

There it is: I tell myself that human nature does not change, and this may be so. I tell myself that the world does not change, and this also may be so: the conditions of existence remain. But for all the comfort such endurance offers, when I face the gulf dividing us, the heart goes out of me. Before the appalling fact of those four millennia and more—one million five hundred and sixty-nine thousand five hundred and so many days from the moment he went into his tomb, so many countable minutes each following each in unbroken succession until the day I came squalling and slippery into life: words desert me.

I know now why they required spells to remember their names in the underworld, why they treasured up spells empowering them to speak. Already before the same void I find myself falling silent. The Summer is upon us; the halls are emptied of students, and the campus has gone lush and quiet. The echo of my footsteps flies down the hallway, fading, and I know that before the Fall term comes, I will follow them.

A word of power. The mind does not reel. A word, we know, has no power. So I once believed. But in a lifetime of research into Egypt, I have become skeptical—unsure of much we in our century take on faith.

I would adduce my reasons; I cannot. A word of power has nothing to do with reason.

Look around you: how much of the power that affects your

life has to do with *reason?* A half-bright undergraduate can tell how long a pebble dropped will fall before it hits the bottom of a well. But not one of my colleagues on the faculty in physics can tell you *why.* Mass attracts mass, they say. Why? Because it does, they aver, uncomfortably echoing Aristotle. If pressed, they will confess it: We don't know *why.*

And so it is, for every phenomenal and noumenal event you name. Trace the chimera Reason to its den, and the ground collapses at your feet. Certain things are. Then they are not. And if, at their beginning and their end, things challenge our sense of how events ought to proceed, the outrage committed against reason is the least of consequences that should concern us.

Evidence, then. On my side of the issue I can produce, as some have already observed, no evidence. I can only suggest, in words, that which I feel with a poignancy that makes all reason hollow, all evidence evanescence, all words the stuff of dream. What I feel, what I know, I cannot speak outright; only sidelong, only glancingly can I tell you what will never be the thing itself.

It has that to do with what you will never know, unless you have, as I, been present at the opening of an Egyptian tomb.

The door is sealed, plastered over from threshold to lintel with a fine, smooth grout, mud of the Nile, the stuff of Chaos itself. In it, one can see the impression of the trowel: here and there the thumbprints of the plasterers, the loops and whorls of their fingerprints intact—fingers that went in time into their own tombs, and moldered into dust—here, still, after five thousand years: you may place your own thumb there, into the lapse of fifty centuries, fit it into the empty socket, filling up the space that once was filled by fingers of a living hand.

Behind the plaster is stone. It comes down, course by uneven course, baulked by oak logs light as balsa now. A haze of dust rises, hovers around you in the stillness, until the moment when your chisel enters the emptiness beyond: a hot, dry air escapes. The tomb has let its final breath at last, as if the one immured within has only now, after long millennia of sleep, given up the ghost.

In a clean tomb, where no water has seeped, the air is adust, and the odor it carries seems to rise from the parching of your own nostrils. In the tombs where rot has entered, that most ravenous of tomb-robbers gusts great squalls of laughter, leaps eagerly to greet you, draw you in to share the sport of its long feast. So it was in Nur-Mar's tomb: at the opening of the probe-hole, the candle we held into the escaping wind died, and the tunnel filled with a horrible presence—not decay, not a smell at all: the presence in the tunnel was sensible only in the hairs it stirred upon our necks.

The clearing of the door told why. Nur-Mar had been buried with an Answerer.

The *ushabti* were, in later dynasties, an artistic convention: small, painted figurines in the image of the deceased and his servants, who were to do for him the onerous labor required in the Duat. They have long fascinated me, in the way all things Egyptian do; the attempt to make literal and concrete what we now conceive as only symbolic: this is essentially Egyptian.

Before the opening of Nur-Mar's tomb, it had never occurred to me to wonder what the origins of this abstracting process might have been in the case of the *ushabti*: if we looked back long enough, would we find the place where art lapses back into the flesh?

The Answerer in Nur-Mar's tomb lay just inside the door. I do not know if there were theoretical or practical reasons for the location. Theoretically, I suppose, stationed near the door an Answerer would be placed so as to intercept anyone who entered with a task for the deceased. Practically, the issue is clearer: whoever stapled his fetters had made certain the chain would stop him short of the offerings of food and wine that filled the chamber just beyond.

There is this quality in any Egyptian tomb: they annihilate time. Whether it is in the clear preservation of the marks left by Nur-Mar's Answerer in his last hours, or in the simple bouquet of dried flowers that we found atop the steward's sarcophagus, in each case, with every trivial find, there is an overwhelming sense that these events stopped only moments before you entered. If the object of Egyptian funerary practice was to preserve the identity (the *Ka*, or *Ba*, or *Kau*, or *Ku*, call it what they would, and did) of the deceased, who is to say they did not succeed? Are there any other faces from the third millennium B.C.E. familiar to us now—not through stone or pigment, but the flesh itself, identifiable and individual, as Ramesses' is in Cairo, or Nur-Mar's is this moment in my memory?

When I was still a boy, almost forty years ago I won, as a prize in a national science competition, a two-week tour of Europe, in company with four dozen other prodigies. My memories of the trip are all decayed now into a series of hotel rooms with exotic fixtures and a damp smell, and a series of interminable bus rides. All lost now, except for one gray, drizzling morning in the valley of the Dordogne, when we descended into the caves of Lascaux. The image of a hand, silhouetted in a haze of charcoal, hangs above me to this day—too high for me to reach. Still I could tell the hand—the left—had been larger than my own. I felt almost a stroke from that hand, a touch on my skin that lingered. I emerged into the gray damp daylight of France and found the surface of the earth a hollow dream.

Never in my life have I felt so utterly alone, a boy of twelve, in a tour bus in Europe, a continent away from a land where I had no home.

As the works of the Egyptians bettered the hunting magic of the Magdalenian—the one hazy image of a hand ramifying, resolving out of chaos to become a face, a body swathed in linen, a room with furniture, almost a life—I am tantalized by the sense that, somewhere in the three millennia of their active seeking, someone in ancient Egypt may have done it. Someone may have reached a hand clear through the rock and pulled himself alive through death's abiding wall.

With classes done, and no research expedition before me, I am reduced to examining a limited body of evidence. I have the lab results before me: copies; the originals the doctor retains, as if jealous of them. They show the chemistry of my blood, the skipping of my heart, the slow, dreaming drift of the EEG. All, the doctor said, were negative. He thinks I am a healthy man.

The X-ray shadows, CT slices, the MR angiograms all show the same object: my skull. The flaring void of nose, wide-staring sockets, the brain behind them in this view only indifferently visible, merely suggested by the net of veins, a fine haze upholding the invisible that is me.

Nothing reveals itself: no tumor sprouting at the center, no erosion mining the stem. I hold the gray films to my desk lamp, and the bright ghost of the bulb hovers a thumb's width away from the obscuration in my eyes.

Nothing is there. But I wonder if, to other eyes, trained in mysteries I do not know, that net of nothing might reveal—what? I do not know, only that the thought of it sends horror through me: fear in my groin, a hand brushing cold up through my viscera. I feel the whispers almost audible, as though dust were blowing already through my heart.

APPLIED AND ENGINEERING PHYSICS

MAXWELL LABS

———— UNIVERSITY

Heard about your news. Think I can help.
Drop by here Fri. aft?
B.

"B" was Budge, who I knew had had his own application in. We are the same vintage, Budge and I, having been hired, reviewed, tenured and promoted in lockstep, as if he were my shadow or I his as we skipped up the steps of academic advancement together. Today I had learned who was whose shadow. Budge, I could tell from what the note did not say, had won his grant. Budge was through the door, and I had simply vanished from the track. Or was about to. When Budge came back from wherever he would spend his grant money, I would not be there to greet him.

This saddened me, more than I would have expected. I have no family, few friends. In my line of work— I cannot blame it on my line of work. But Budge and I, although our shared interests are few, and he has his family and his work beside, Budge and I have shared something like friendship this past decade. If friendship is the expectation that a certain face and voice will be there, met by chance and passed as easily, that was what we had. At the thought that one of our faces would be missing, I found myself growing what may have even approximated affection for Budge.

But that note! The cheery briskness of it—so like him, and so unlike my mood. *Thought he could help.* With what, friend B.? For a moment the exception I had made for Budge broke down, and I included him in my resentment against the well-funded world of the (as they like to say) hard sciences. I tossed the wad of paper in a corner of my office, and strode angrily out of doors.

none who is outside know this spell, for it is a great mystery. Thou shalt not perform this in the presence of any person except thyself alone, for it is indeed an exceedingly great mystery which no man whatever knoweth.

These are the words of power to be spoken alone for entering into the underworld like a god. Thou shalt not speak these words, nor cause them to be spoken, in the presence of any person, for they are a great mystery, and the eye of no man soever must see them, for it is a thing of abomination for every man to know it. Hide it, therefore; the Book of the Lady of the Hidden Temple is its name.

—They're in what? Astronomy? Agronomy you say, oh dear. Were their shoes clean? They won't start tilling up the back yard, will they? What? Nematodes? They're little worms, I think. Well I don't think worms are preferable to animals, no.

I could hear Budge sigh, and then silence, cut through by a tiny insect's voice. When it was still at last Budge spoke again.

—Fly out? I don't think— Yes, you're right, I will be the one to complain if it's a sty. The schools? Oh, I'd forgotten, they're coming too, aren't they. We could board— You spoke with them about it? And they? Oh. Like that. My idea? Well I suppose you're right it was.

Another sigh. At my ear I heard impatient whispering, but I lingered at the door, listening, as if the sounds coming through the door were smells and I was hungry.

—Dear? I'm terribly sorry to have left you with all this. I can see what a bother. Well I'm done now, you know. Yes, just this morning, yes, and you should see! You'd like that? Yes, I can, but what I wanted to say was I can take all this household-packing— Yes, all of it, of course. Tonight? Oh, that would be lovely, yes. I'll make the reservations. Celebrate your emancipation, yes. And my success, all right if you insist. Well then: until this evening?

A brief, intimate kiss against the receiver, and then the sound of the one kissed being cradled. Another sigh. I knocked.

—What? What?

Furniture moved, journals falling slapped the floor, and then the door opened wide. Budge was in the doorway waving his limbs, beside himself with anxious hospitality.

— Oh, ——, it's you, so glad you could come I'm terribly sorry I heard it on the grapevine don't you know, no don't sit over there it will fall over sit here, yes, I think it's a terrible thing but don't get excited I happened to call the Foundation this morning to clear something up and I asked, naturally, after you, assuming you had one too, just wanted to spread the jolly around, you know, and imagine my surprise. I was quite cool with him, but I gather there's no appeal, nothing to do until next year, hmm? anyhow I say are you all right?

A cold blush had flowed up out of my chest as I sat down. For a moment, Budge vanished in a gray, humming haze. Words may have come out of my mouth, something about the stairs.

—Those infernal elevators again. Stuck on the sixteenth floor I don't doubt. Always carting something in or out up in plasma physics, though why they need both at once I can't understand. Keeps you fit, though, climbing up and down, don't you think?

He waved his arms and inhaled. —Feeling better?

I leaned back, feeling the resentment that had brought me in evaporate, diffusing into that chill sweat fuming off my scalp. I waved a deprecatory hand.

—Good. He bounced up from his chair again, caromed off the corners of the room. —I'm so glad you made it over, you see. I'd almost forgotten. Up to here—he sliced a palm-edge across his neck—with packing and such.

He ricocheted to a storage cabinet, drummed resonantly within, emerged trailing wires like mummy-cloths.

—Oh yes of course you, you're the lucky one, none of this domestic clutter, just jetting off to the Nile whenever— He stopped, clapping a hand over his mouth. —Oh dear fellow I'm sorry of course you can't. I mean you think you can't now, don't you?

His voice dropped to a whisper. —But that's what I want to talk to you about.

With an absurd pantomime of caution he eased his short, round form over to the door. Closing it softly, turning his back against it, arms spread from jamb to jamb, he leaned out toward me, and hissed, —Mum's the word. Eh?

I must have goggled at him, apparently the correct response, for a look of satisfaction, turning his ordinarily pleasant face into something terribly reminiscent of a fed pig, spread upward from the discrete knob of his chin until his eyes half closed. He scampered back to his desk, spread a trough through the mounded printouts and journals, and funneled a conspiratorial gaze down its length.

—Your grant: What were you going to spend it on? What's the expensive part? Eh?

Before I could think, he answered for me.

—Labor, eh? Equipment, eh? *Time*. All that digging around. And why? *Because you don't know where to look*.

I drew back, wondering suddenly how much he knew: with Nur-Mar's scroll, I did know where to look—within five miles or so. With proper funding, with luck, I might have found the site within four seasons.

—But what if you knew?

His face was lost in darkness, his arms waving around a pulsing void.

—What if you *knew*, I say? Knew *exactly*.

I may have murmured something weakly. I felt weak.

—*Precisely*. Budge surged on, caught up in the glory of his idea. —Where. To. Look. I've read your work. There's always an entrance passage, yes? With a door, heaped up with rubble, just a few meters below the surface. Right?

I nodded.

—And what if you could point at a spot in the ground, and tell your man, —There: right there. You dig down until you strike a door, and then let me know. Eh? And it was really there? No guessing? You just go back to your tent and fan yourself while they dig a simple little pit. Do it yourself, if you had to. None of that trenching this way and that, all that blind rooting about. Eh? What then? How much will your expedition cost then?

I didn't believe a word of it—he was babbling from the abysmal depths of ignorance, I knew—but even so I was terribly excited. What would such an expedition cost? If I could find the entrance right away? I could hire a single fellah for a month for less than the cost of a night in Cairo.

And once I was in?

—Oh, I know, once you're in you'll need equipment—I know you you fox, you're on to something big I can tell—once you're in you'll need your local bearers, trucks, all that preservation gear.

He waved a hand airily toward the door. —But that's the beauty of it, don't you see? Once you need all that, the bloody foundations will be falling all over each other with their money. Hah! Let 'em! You know what we can tell them: Put it where the sun don't shine! Eh?

The vision of it opened up before me then, exactly as if the door had rolled away: not prized down stone by stone, but hinged, noiselessly opening for me—for me alone. Budge was right: if I only knew where to start, I wouldn't need the elaborate support an exploratory dig requires. But he was wrong as well. Once I was in that door, I would need no help from anyone, ever again. Let the trash and glitter go to ruin. I would be—

I would be a damned fool, I realized, to go on thinking this way. I could no more tell the exact location of the entrance than I could speak the name of the King.

—Ah, I know. You're thinking old Budge has dropped a bearing somewhere, am I right? Fused my logic circuits, yes? Ho ho, my friend, just you wait and see.

He straightened, and glanced around the cramped and cluttered office.

—But remember, he hissed. —Mum's the word.

The Papyrus of ——, who draws the horizon over him a living god: the Papyrus whereby he stablisheth his name, whereby all names before his are naught: where

While the nurse's back was turned, I snatched the folder, vanished through the door. An empty corridor; an elevator at my elbow gaped, the doors quivered and I leapt in. Dim in brushed chrome, my reflection hunched over a brown square of manila. The thing itself was in my hands. Pink carbon sheets, a sheaf of gray transparencies: I recoiled.

What had I been thinking of? Did I really think that doing away with the evidence would help me now? And if I was caught, what better way to make it public—to spread it far beyond my doctor's office? Had he returned yet, and found me missing? Had he summoned the police?

The elevator halted: I stepped out, alone in a long hallway. Doors opened on blank corridors; down one hall they all stood open, and in each a small child lay inside a bird-cage, suspended above the floor. At the end I faced a wall of glass, and beyond it cribs and incubators, the dreaming reach of small arms, of feet thrust out falling slowly down.

My anxiety returned. The nurse had discovered the theft; police were seeking me at this moment. I turned, walking quickly, blindly down inconclusive corridors, the envelope clutched at my chest. At a door labeled NECROPSY I shied away, clattered down a flight of stairs (the elevators were a trap), and out into bedlam.

Three ambulances crowding the entrance, hatches open and disgorging three clusters of pale green attendants, flash of chrome and white, an arm asplay, a shocking blot of red. As I watched, my back against the door through which I had emerged, more figures in green converged on each sprawl- ing form until the red was obscured entirely, and each cluster started moving, like a swarm of bees deciding, of a moment, to fly in my direction.

And in the center of the nearest swarm, pale and deathly still, I saw the face of Budge.

The air in the viewing room was immaculately cool, faultlessly clean, perfectly unperfumed. There was a gathering of fam- ily seated by the door, receiving the murmurs of the guests. A gloved hand lay limp in mine a moment, some words may have passed. The hand, the words, and I drifted along the edges of the room.

I looked back at the mourners. None seemed substantial, compared with the mountain of gleaming flesh heaped on the dais. Budge shone beneath the sourceless light, so bright he seemed some cinematic trick of projection: I half expected him to dissolve as I approached. But he remained, the husk of him, eyes stiffly shuttered, lips pursed as if disdaining their overlay of rouge. Absolutely still, absolutely absent.

There was a beating somewhere in my skull, a dry pressure about my eyes. The image of Budge's face vanished into a pool of darkness.

I am —— the great one, son of no one, to whom was given his head after it had been cut off. I have knit together my bones; I have made myself whole and sound; I have become young once more; I am ——, Lord of Eternity.

I uttered mine own name and I was born, Khep-era-Thoth, who rolls his own name before him, lord of divine words, lord of books and master of speech, possessor of all knowledge human and divine.

I will do away the evil by the word of my mouth: Obey me, demon of sickness, demon of blood, abomination of the unclean. I possess my own name, mightier than thine. Yea, the secret of my birth I hold in my mouth. Obey me!

Begone, unclean thing of filth and pus! Begone, for my *ba* is stablished by the word of my mouth, yea, before my mouth it stablished my mouth.

Unclean thing of blood and filth, thy name is nothing.

I awoke in the dark, the bare room around me awash in whispers.

I could not see.

I heard the curtains sigh, felt them brushing my face where I lay. I could smell; there had been rain in the night. With a rush of fear I thought it might be morning, light lying all around me blind, and I sat up in bed, flung my arms out before me. The curtain passed again across my face, and this time I could see its pale folds. Against the dim angles of the walls, beside the darkness of the open closet, I could make out the faint, flurried pulsation of that deeper darkness, still constricted to a moon-sized disc.

What had awakened me?

There had been a voice, speaking close in my ear a single word that took forever to announce.

I imagined it was the voice of Budge, but I knew it was not: no ghosts trouble my sleep. But there is something other than ghosts. Something older, perhaps, of which ghosts are but an echo. I am certain of this, although I know not what it is. I know only that a voice was speaking, close in my ear, a word whose syllables I might almost recall. But what the word, and whence the voice, still I cannot say.

What profit hath a man of all his labor which he taketh away under the sun?

One generation passeth away, and another cometh: but earth abideth forever.

All the rivers run into the sea; yet the sea is not full; unto the place from whence the rivers come, thither they return again.

All things are full of labor; man cannot utter it: the eye is not satisfied with seeing, or the ear filled with hearing.

The voice of the preacher rustled at graveside, withering in the sun that glared down on the thin, dark figures gathered around. In the heat they wavered as if about to fall. Iris Budge stood nearby; her eldest son, a thinner, taller, pale caricature of Budge, held an umbrella over his mother's head; he had neglected to shelter himself, and in the premature June heat his red hair clung limp on his forehead; a drop of moisture gleamed at the pinched nose; his eyes were slitted in the intense, inward brooding of adolescence. Not Mrs. B.: throughout the service (saving only the moment when she raised her eyes to stare at me) she gazed, a bit vaguely, on the gleaming shell before her. I blocked her behind a disc of black, the better to compose my face.

The small gathering dispersed, threading outward through the maze of stones and obelisks, leaving behind them the unbearably sleek casket. I stopped, and let the few mourners behind me pass. Back at the grave, the casket had vanished into its socket; the vivid yellow of a backhoe shimmered, its single arm gesturing toward the grave. A half-dozen figures remained, looking from the distance like a group of clay figures. The urge to walk back almost got the better of me, but I stood, held by the shreds of civility that linger, even at the graveside. I knew I could not wait, but I could not imagine how to phrase my request. It would sound selfish. But *I* was dying: surely they would—

How long I might have wavered there, shimmering in indecision, I do not know: two figures, a short and a tall, detached themselves and walked toward me.

Vaults quiver,
Earth's bones tremble,
At seeing ——— rise as power,
Whose mother knows not his name;
Who eats her entrails where he had his name,
Who eats the elder gods when they come, their
    bodies full of magic,
From the Isle of Flames.

I have another memory of Professor ———, dead now these twenty years. He was old when we first met, five years away from retirement, but still hale enough to climb with me on Khufu's pyramid when he took me with him on his annual expedition to the el Amarna site. My first trip to Egypt was his last; a stroke the month after our return left one side of his body useless, and made his last ten years a cage, in which he struggled to organize the notes of his last dig.

The last time we met the month was May, my dissertation was back from the bindery, and in a week I was to be a doctor of philosophy. I had emerged from the library startled to find the sun warm on my head, the air alive with spring, and my feet reluctant at the turning of his gate. To spend an hour or two of a day like this indoors in the company of an invalid seemed suddenly odious.

His attendant, an old woman (so I thought—she may have

been fifty) who silently dusted his notes without dislodging them, who pushed his wheelchair, and, I suspected, shared his bed, led me to his study. He was shriveled on the sagging vinyl slings of the chair, slumped over to his dead side, examining, under an illuminated magnifier, an ordinary page of print. He had gone almost entirely deaf as well, so I do not know by what means the old woman caused him to turn as we entered. Then she was gone and he was fussing with the switch to turn off the magnifier.

He was embarrassed as I found it for him, and to get past the moment I shouted, —I brought you something. I produced a copy of my dissertation. The smile that had tugged painfully at half his face softened, and his good eye wandered.

—Thank you, he whispered, slurring. —I can't read it now, you know.

—You read most of it.

—Yes. But it's done now. It's— He groped for a word, the hand on his lap twitching. —Finished.

He sank farther into the chair, air escaping from somewhere. His hand passed vaguely over the chaos on his desk, the typewriter, dust-covered, beside him.

Embarrassed at the implied self-pity, I shouted at him, —But you didn't read all of it.

The eyebrow on the good side rose. I wondered if that had always been a gesture of his, or if behind the nerveless face he was trying to raise them both.

—Before I bound it I added one more chapter. The committee never saw it.

I placed the book on his desk; it slid an inch or two down a slope of index cards, then lay still. —I'll tell you what it says.

With his good hand he reached across his potbelly, retrieved his left from where it had fallen. He folded them together and closed his eyes. —Tell me. The voice seemed to come from a distance.

—It's only a theory, really. An appendix to my thesis, with a research program to prove it out: sites, classes of artifact, periods, all that. But the theory's the thing—

I stopped myself from adding, —And it will make me famous. I told my suspicions instead, and my voice was shaking as I spoke, quivering with the relief that at last I had called up the courage to tell. I told him of the conviction that had grown in me, over the two years of my dissertation research, through the waste hours when the labor was painful. I told him of my vision of a king, my first, naive conception of the King: a builder perhaps, who rescued his people from a period of chaos, brought the Black Land out of darkness. His people worshipped him, but then something happened. Some tragedy struck: madness, perhaps, the particular curse of kings. Madness, and his benign rule turned to tyranny, his people's awe now underwritten by fear. Perhaps he had closed the temples, as the heretic Amenhotep IV would a millennium later.

He nodded slowly once, without looking up, just before a spasm passed silently over half his face. I stopped, wondering what it meant, unable to guess what emotion might be stirring in a man about to die, alone and in obscurity, listening to a young man outline a program for professional immortality.

—Obviously, I went on, my voice already assuming the tone of the incipient lecturer, —there must be more to the story. Apostasy, even in a king, is not enough to drive his survivors to efface all record of his rule: our picture of the Nineteenth

Dynasty, after all, is clear enough. He did something, this king, that so outraged or frightened them that they felt even his name to be a menace, not to be suffered to survive. And finally all memory of him, everything he had done or touched, seen or heard—everything was destroyed. Not an echo of his reign comes down to our time. Only this complete break in the record. But what was it? What dangerous madness could so seduce a king?

I stopped, my mouth a desert. His face was carefully neutral. I took a breath, and then I launched out upon the silence.

—What if this king had set out to learn the Word of Power, the word Thoth whispered in the ear of Ptah when between the two of them they made the world? I am convinced it happened, inevitably, in a land so obsessed with the supernatural: one rose up among them who personified their dream. And though of course—

My voice cracked. I knew what I must say here, but even then something in me rebelled.

—Of course there could be no such word, no power to create a world, not really. So there must have been something else, some physical sign for such a word, a substitute. By that material logic they always used to deal with the abstract, he must have built that world himself, a tomb-burial to beggar all the tombs since Menes founded the First Dynasty. That must have been it, you see: it would follow from all the Egyptian practices we know, only raised to such an extreme—an inevitable extreme, you see—that he had to ransack the kingdom to supply it. We can imagine the rationale. The Word of Power needs its own perfect seat, the proper circumstances, a temple within which its own prophet-priest the King would guard the Word, and finally at the appointed time utter it, and then the world would change, all Egypt would be transported bodily into the afterlife and death's dominion would become the King's.

—Imagine what power such a fantasy would give him over his people. How great an effort he could have extracted by the mere promise alone: if the nation had bent all its efforts toward the construction of a mere pyramid, not once but repeatedly in the preceding dynasty, how would they devote themselves to a sovereign who promised to bring them all within his horizon, and make the gates of death turn back upon themselves? How hard they must have worked!

—And how violently, in the end, they rebelled. The labor was too great, even for the promised end. Or perhaps they revenged themselves upon him only after he died, and they realized that he had failed? Maybe that explains the revulsion: among a people for whom belief in magic was essential to life, what if one of them set out to put that magic to some ultimate test? How savagely would they have turned to tear him when he fell?

—I have only to look, and I know I can find it, the one thing absolutely necessary. The tomb. The greatest tomb in the history of Egypt: the greatest find in the history of Egyptology. For it must be there. I am convinced it was not rifled. That's the beauty of it, you see: if the tomb had been found, if such a quantity of goods and artifacts as it must have contained had been released, the world would be littered with evidence of his reign—and we have none! And even had there been some attempt to destroy them, the signs would still be there: records of Radedef survived the destruction of his monuments, and he was nothing to this one. I am certain of it: the King was sealed in his horizon, and they threw away the key. Perhaps they even imprisoned him in it still living. Who knows—

I stopped, finding myself teetering again on the verge of something disastrous, recognizing something in myself trying to make itself heard. I had wanted to go on, to explain where I thought this tomb might be, how best to start the search. But in the midst of that explanation I sensed a desire I had theretofore not known: a desire, almost a conviction, that in his tomb I should find the King himself, still living, and from his lips would hear—everything. The truth about everything Egyptian, about a world lost long before I was born, the truth about— even then I did not know just what I hoped to hear.

I held my tongue. Silence, like a thickening of dust. Professor —— was still, his hands carefully motionless, his expression inscrutable: I felt myself teetering, a scale waiting to tip with the next weight placed upon the pan. —Imagine evidence, I cried. —Texts, artifacts, everything perfectly preserved, from a crisis early on, at the very heart of the Egyptian social, political, and religious complex. At the origins of our own—

I was shouting, I realized, a foot from the old man's face, as if volume could give substance to my words; shouting into a face that seemed, more and more as I peered into it, too uniformly relaxed.

—He's dead, I whispered, and my voice fell hoarse among the echoes fading in the quiet room. I reached out and laid a hand upon his shoulder. His head lolled, his jaw opened, and a rattling snore escaped.

He recovered, one half of his face blinking and rewrinkling as he tried to lift both hands to rub his eyes. —xcuse me. He muttered at last. —m sorry. Sleep again. No reflection, please blieve me.

He settled his glasses on his nose and his living hand upon his paunch. —Would you mind terribly much repeating?

I put the cassette in the slot, and clunked its hatch down:

Budge's voice emerged, attenuated, as if it really were a spirit's voice.

—Sorry to leave this to last minutes, ———, but I'm all at sixes and sevens with this and that. I'm packing books with both hands while I talk. I don't know, Lester, ask your mother. Now. Assuming the beastly custodials haven't changed the locks overnight, you should find the thing on the shelves to the right of the door as you face it. From inside, that is. It's about the size of a carry-on bag. Black leatherette. Do you have it? Careful when you lift it down: it's not terribly fragile but it is heavy, and I don't want you to break your foot. Now.

Now. Budge's voice went on, brightly and (I could tell) well pleased with himself—with his packing, his ingenuity, his casual belief that somewhere he was still alive. In his empty office, the familiar clutter had been reduced to stripped shelves, a few mounds of equipment catalogs and boxes of bright electronic shards. His voice was almost unbearably real to me, bouncing sharply from the bare walls as I acted out his instructions, levered down the heavy case and thumbed up its hasps, muttering to myself the instructions from the tape. My hands were trembling too much to attach the power lines to the battery, and I had to stop, shutting off the tape-player with more effort than necessary.

Sitting at the bare table beside the open case, for a long time I could not catch my breath. I was near to crying. Not for Budge: do not mistake me, it was none of that. A wordless despair had seized me, and was long minutes vanishing back into whatever pit it had crept out of.

I had started to believe in Budge's absurd promise.

When I could take a breath without its catching, I eased down the button on the recorder, and turned again to my inheritance. At his direction I flipped three switches, waited for the screen to light and settle, a flickering void, then set two dials at his instructions.

The screen shuddered.

I was looking at a luminous floor plan of the lobby, six stories below my feet: there was the ugly aluminum sculpture, there the three broad granite steps up from the entrance, the inscribed marble benches, the men's and ladies' with their pipes and porcelain off on either side. At my ear, Budge was explaining how it worked, but I couldn't hear: my eyes were full, and my heart was beating loudly. At the center of the screen, a darkness beat as well.

There were small rites to perform. I carried my files—on the King, on myself—out into the back yard. There was a barbecue pit there, relic of an earlier tenant.

I had thought so much tinder would flare in an instant, flash and vanish, but the burning was slow: one page at a time caught at the corners, the blue flame flickering as it read over, consumed, and curled each up to reveal the next: I saw a story roll up like the sky at Judgment Day, blacken to ashes before my eyes. This was on Wednesday.

On Thursday I drove to the school where I had taken my doctor's degree. My thesis was shelved among a thousand like it in the doctoral papyrus dump. As I pulled it from the shelf and felt again its ungainly mass, like no other book in the world, in the solitude of the library I felt as if my adult life had been a dream: here I was carrying my new dissertation into the library, about to walk to Professor ———'s.

The circulation clerk took my name and address, and accepted my alien faculty ID. I hoped urgently she would not notice the names on the card and the book were the same. As she opened my thesis to stamp the date due, she spoke.

—You're the first one to check this out in . . . thirty years.

—Someone else checked it out?

—Sure. See? She showed me the dim, purple date, two weeks after I had received my degree.

—Who?

A laugh. —Thirty years ago? I wasn't even born.

I stood facing the house that had been Professor ———'s.

The housekeeper-nurse had inherited, I remembered. I had never learned her name. Was she still there? In the bowels of the house, a bell rang; footsteps approached; the door swung back. An ordinary woman, far too young, holding a wide-eyed infant.

———

AND ONE OTHER thing: as I drove out of town, over the bridge where the breath of the sea blew in through the window, over the rail I heaved the black flapping shape of my thesis. It dropped from sight, and I could only imagine the splash.

This vignette represents the deceased on his knees, embracing his soul.

I looked around me, and there was nothing more to do: no family for farewells, no friends; my equipment I carried in my own hands. My office I simply locked, and in my empty house I locked my keys. Let the newspapers gather, the mail spill out of its box. I wished for the days of milk delivery, that one more mourner might leave offerings at my tomb. No matter: I would be gone—escaped—into darkness or into light.

of the ashes is the soul reborn in the twelfth hour of the Duat. He enters the tail of the mighty serpent, which is named Divine Life, and issues from its mouth in the form of the scarab Khepera, who rolls his own egg of spittle and mud. But the last door of all is guarded by Isis, she who nurses the throne, and by Nephthys, the barren one who wails, and they also are in the form of serpents; their mouths

are open, their tails twine together, their fangs drip
venom as the soul of the deceased approaches.

Now Urnes, the river of Duat, flows into the
primeval

I awoke once, en route, in the never-never-time of the Atlan-
tic: over the wing the sun was rising, spreading purple shadows
miles across the clouds. The cabin was quiet but for the vibration of the engines, the rushing of wind, the intermittent snore
of my two-hundred-some companions. I thought I saw a small
beetle, gold and iridescent blue, emerge from the carpeting at
my feet. It raised its wingcovers, and flew a yard or two down
the aisle before disappearing into the center of my vision.

A voice rose and subsided, murmured, surged and submerged
again, out of and into the eastward urging of the engines: *unun
neb-t shet-t unun maa-t; unun neb-t shet-t; unun neb-t upsh; neh-ti neheh;
unun neb-t upsh, upsh, upshhhhhhh.*

At Cairo airport, I had nothing to declare.

The long duration of an afternoon that should have been night
I kept to my room, the curtains drawn against the glare. My

window faced west, and as the afternoon wore thin and finally unraveled, the curtains caught cold fire; the window was a blaze of gauzy orange, reddening. In the midst of the glow, a black circle pulsing. Outside, in the heat and light, cars gathered, bleating. I lay and watched the pulsating void, listened to the thread of beeps and baas, and in the distance, on a wire stretched somewhere in the recesses of my skull, a thin voice was chanting.

The room was red and dim around me, and the voice had somehow escaped into the evening, where it ululated across the domed and minareted roof of Cairo: evening prayer. I stumbled from the bed and threw the curtains open. Beyond the new city the Nile shimmered around Rawdah. Beyond lay Al Jizah, where I told myself I could see the buildings of the University, where Professor —— and I had stayed the first evening of my first trip into Egypt. And beyond Al Jizah, black against the blue-green-gold of the horizon, the Pyramids.

I could not see the Sphinx, but I knew where it lay, could conjure up the blind face of Khafre staring back at me. Blind, and crumbling, and slumping back into the sand.

I drew the curtain across the glass: for a moment my face, pale, gleamed back at me, one arm reaching out from the darkness.

The riddle of the Sphinx—the real riddle, the real Sphinx—is that we do not know the question.

I rented a Rover through the auspices of the Egyptian Auto Club, located conveniently around the corner from the Museum where the relics of Nur-Mar rest. I did not pay the visit. In my two days remaining in Cairo, I made three stops. One to the Etymological Society, up the broad contorted snake of Ramesses Street. I brought with me some copies I had sketched of some of the later marks from Nur-Mar's papyrus which still perplexed me. I hoped they would perplex them as well.

My credentials were enough to grant me entry to the Director, a fellow who, behind two solar discs of eyeglasses, looked a bit like Gandhi. He peered with his magnifiers at my sketches, and then looked up at me with the same abstracted stare.

—Where did you get these?

I told him something like the truth. He remembered the excavation, of course; the glyphs had been printed on the seals of certain jars, I said. It is easy to lie, to lie gracefully I find, when the face of your listener is hidden in a pool of black. I heard a slow exhalation, a dusty sigh, and when I looked sidelong he had removed his glasses to rub his eyes.

—We see so many of these, he said.

My heart almost stopped. The darkness in my eyes went gray.

—And it's always the same. The man sighed again over my sketches, and replaced the glasses; his eyes flashed large, as if he had seen something important. A momentary distortion.

For a long minute he gazed up at the ceiling, where the fan was slowly threshing flies. —They never stopped, you see. You must know something of that yourself. They never stopped adding in. Any time they thought of something new, they simply reached into air and added on another glyph. It's worse than chaos, he sighed. — It's infinity. It comes to the same thing in the end, doesn't it?

He slumped, if this were possible, deeper in the dim brown heat, the rumples on his suit creasing through his face. — Did you know? I was trained as a chemist. For one year at University, before Nasser. Then the revolution came, and my family left, and I could study anything I wanted. We were all nationalists then, you know—very much so. And I decided that our heritage, our glorious gift to the human race, would be the more fitting study. But today— He pushed the scrap of paper back toward me. —Today I feel nostalgic for the benzene ring. You know the ring? A snake that bites its tail. That is perfection—none of this ringing in of signs from here and there and tomorrow: just carbon and hydrogen making geometry together.

—No. I am sorry, Doctor ——: I cannot help you. I hope it was not important.

My second visit was to the Egyptian Library, and my work there was all in solitude, and all deliciously null.

And finally to the tourism board, where nothing consequential happened.

I am convinced more and more each day that I am dying. I left Cairo over the El Giza bridge, the bright Nile counterfeiting the morning sun. As I waited in the traffic in the Shari Al-Haram to make the left turn that would take me down to Route ø2, around me roared an endless procession of tourist buses, their windows black to opacity. What convinces me of my own hastening end is not the omnipresence of death around me—as I waited, a dog wandered into the traffic, rolled once as it was hit, righted itself, then went down again and was still—what convinces me is the persistence of my memory, as it replays before me isolated fragments of my life.

The struggle of the dog to right itself I had seen before, from behind the wheel of a '58 Chevrolet on the boulevard that circled the city where I grew up. It was my car that struck the dog the second time—I could feel the thump of something solid beneath my feet, a brief rumbling roll, and then the motionless shape receding in the rearview mirror. I had refused to drive for a week after that, and my foster parents, angry—self-doubt they could never tolerate, I think because it confirmed their own uncertainty about me—threatened to revoke my driving privileges. And that dog—those dogs, the one warm beneath the Egyptian sun, the other still receding in the mirror—those dogs coalesce into a third, the one another set of parents had given me the week of my arrival in their home. I was twelve, I think, and alone in the house when a strange car stopped at the door, a woman handed me the collar with an aggrieved, —She ran out so fast.

The problem of digging a hole: twice I laid her in it, and twice I had to lift her out again and dig it deeper.

Within a year I was watching the since-familiar backhoe perform its obsequies over an equally parching soil, the thin blue of its exhaust the smoke of some small incineration as it backed the dust over that set of foster parents. Their car had been pinned beneath a bus. And in every case—I am omitting others—what struck me most was an emptiness in the visible world, a quality of light like the echo in an empty house, in every scene once inhabited by the—

What convinces me that I am dying is the way I maunder on, about dead pets, and foster parents, and myself. It is as if I have grown old—and I am not yet fifty. But these memories will not abate—they quicken, as if some part of myself hastens to become empty.

Come then, Thoth, provided with charm, quicker than greyhounds, fleeter than light. I am Khepera who produced himself upon the let of his mother. Untie the bandages, twice, which fetter my mouth. Behold, I collect the charm from the one with whom it abides, creating the gods from silence, giving the mother-heat to the gods, making forms of existence from the thigh of thy mother. Behold, this charm is given me from where it is, quicker than greyhounds, fleeter than light, more solid than shadow.

I have called it a tomb. More and more I doubt that is the proper term for the structure I seek. But I am yet baffled by what to call it: his retreat? his sanctuary? his redoubt? My horizon, the Nur-Mar Papyrus calls it, as it tallies the expense, the laborers and their rations, the sleds of undressed stone removed, the blocks brought in. My horizon: so all the kings, from the Third Dynasty on, referred to the tombs they prepared; here was the gate through which they would pass, like the sun at evening, into the land of the night. And like the sun, the term implied, the king would rise again.

Aahku-t ——, the papyrus calls it: the horizon of the nameless one; *Aakhu-t heh*, the eternal horizon, the tomb: *Aakhu-t sheta-t, shet-t metcha*: the secret horizon where the writing is read, as near as I can translate it: a word has been struck from the end of the phrase, and the last word could also be the word for a cutting tool, the verb "to destroy," the name of a god, or an edict, decree, liturgy, book, writing, letter. And late in the papyrus, a new sign inserts itself into the sequence: "navel-of-the world" might be one reading: "bottomless pit" another; but an alternative reading, not entirely to be dismissed, is "noisome and trackless swamp." In the last occurrence, the phrase seems to have become nonsense: I cannot interpret the glyphs, read them frontward or backward as I might.

Whatever he called it, for whatever purpose, it is clear that he intended to enter it, and I find no indication that he was going to wait to die before he did. His redoubt, I have come to call it, for it seemed that, in the final period of his reign, he felt pressed: the size of the work crew doubles, then doubles again. In the last year of its construction, perhaps forty thou-

sand labored on the site; all, it seems, slaves from a country
I have never heard of, and perhaps never existed: the name
given in the papyrus is the word for "mute," a class of servant
employed in sensitive tasks, for which they qualified by having undergone glossectomy. In these passages, the handwriting
hastens, slurs to hieratic, and the tale of construction stresses
the speed urged on the crews. The work goes on—indeed its
pace quickens, and the quantities of stone shifted, the provi-
sions and furnishings crafted and stored, assume such mag-
nitude that one cannot but doubt that the hyperbole typical
of such accounts is at work: if the blocks involved are even a
tenth the size of those from which the Pyramids were built,
the manuscript describes a quarry large enough to produce a
mountain range of Pyramids.

Then—curiously—the work of the construction, the physical details of it, disappear from the text, as if the decree of
silence has caused the laborers to vanish. Perhaps the work was
finished. There is no telling. The narrative breaks off with the
phrase, "And then I caused—" I caused: *ta un*; or the phrase
may be *ta hep,* to hide, or *ta hems,* to dwell, to make inhabited.
I caused, I had, I made habitable my horizon, my secret horizon of the cutting tool; I sank into the noisome and trackless
swamp. A rebus that re-forms itself upon each reading; it is a
translator's nightmare.

With Budge's device mounted beside me in the Rover I drove
out into the desert, the screen flickering, distracting me from

my road with glimpses of shapes moving beneath the ground—
large, vague masses of rock sliding beneath rock. I don't know
to what use he intended to put his creation, but for me it was
an answer out of a dream, removing every obstacle between me
and my goal. And as I left populated roads, then roads entirely
behind me, I knew that I had entered into a new epoch in
Egyptology.

Three days I drove the upper reaches of the Valley and
beyond, three days of wild shocks that I still feel echoing in my
bones, of sun that blinded me, and sand that filled my mouth
with the arid taste of my youth, the taste of Egypt, and I drove
on. The whisper in my ear was urgent behind me; I drove on
into the darkness that formed always ahead and always out of
reach. On the second day, I bit my tongue clear through, spit
the tip of it into the wind and drove on, mouth filling with salt
and the sharp taste of pain.

A dozen, two dozen, half a hundred undiscovered tombs
flickered on the screen as I rode over them with my wheels:
small tombs, large tombs, tombs plain and elaborate of form,
but nothing answered the size, the majesty, the ineffable difference that I would know in the one I sought.

On the evening of the third day, after the shadow of the
Horn had climbed the eastern sky, half-maddened by three
days' search, I found it.

The image was vague, as if lying at a great depth, or in a
stratum of rock less lucid than the rest. But it could be nothing
other than the tomb of him I sought: Vast, it seemed a map of
a world unrolled beneath me, bafflingly intricate, tantalizingly
obscure.

So much I saw on first glance, and came near to flipping the Rover as I applied the brakes: I turned a full circle in the sand before stopping, one wheel slightly bent by a boulder. I restarted, moving slowly by headlight up and down the slope, from the base of the jagged cliff behind me to the rim where the plain fell steeply toward the Nile, trying to assemble a clearer map of the subsurface.

No clearer, except at

I have made my way.
I know thee and I know thy name.
Thy name is ——, the unsounded,
Yea, who spake thy own name.
No things are unseen to the one who is unseen;
No names are unknown to the one whose name is
    nought.
I know thee and I know thy name.
Thy name is ——.
Thy name is *Ami-seshet*;
Thanassa-Thanassa is thy name.
Thy name is *Arethikasathaka*;
Npthysysiseremhesihrahaputchetef is thy

—I am a shepherd, sah.
—But you have no sheep.
My tongue, thick and bleeding, would barely form the words.

—This is true, sah. They are in the hills.

He waved a robed arm off to the darkened west, where I had thought only the Libyan desert lay. —With my son. I have come into the Valley for work.

I nodded and said nothing. At the word "work," he had tried to catch my eyes: his were black pits, unfathomable beneath a ragged burnoose. In the white glare of the lantern, his face was half extinguished. The silence between us stretched, until I made an unnecessary adjustment to the lantern, which gave a popping noise and went out.

—That is better, sah.

The bedouin leaned back, and sighed as if he had made himself more comfortable against the rock. Again the silence returned, and with it my fear. Watching him settle, I realized I had held the same half-crouch since his arrival; my pen still poised over my notebook where I had been jotting—creature of habit—notes about the site. I folded the notebook, and snapped it in my shirt-pocket. I don't know what became of the pen.

The man's eyes followed my every move, two gleams shifting in two black pits. I wanted to keep him talking. Why, I didn't know, only that it calmed me to hear him speak, and everything I learned about him helped me to believe he meant no harm. Under the sun, with the tourist buses winding through the gullies below, he would have seemed nothing more than an Arab shepherd. Now the boundaries of the known had shrunk to the sphere of a Coleman lantern's light—and now even that had collapsed upon itself, leaving me outside. In the dark he became by turns a thief, a brigand, a ghost, a djinn, and then things for which I had no name.

—How long have you been a shepherd then?

The question sounded foolish to me—incongruous with the time and place. Of course he had been a shepherd as long as he could remember, and his father before him, and so on. But to my surprise he answered eagerly.

—Ah. You see very well. I was not always a shepherd. I was son of a—how is it?—holy man, yes? A mullah, you understand? Not one of these ignorant dervishes that come from the east, no, or a bedouin madman with visions of the Prophet, none of these. He was an educated man. Was his mistake.

The robed arm swept off to the north, the sleeve breathing a dry odor of sheep. —We lived in a modern house in the city. Electric lights. Plumbing. There was a clock to tell the time for prayers: it knew the phases of the moon. The muezzin had a microphone. All of these things, and my family as well. My brothers and sisters. One mother.

He picked up a handful of sand, and let it slip between his fingers. The night breeze drew it out in a curtain, gauzy under the light of the stars. —My brothers, I do not know what became of them. My sisters and myself they put into the street. My mother— A long sigh escaped him, as if his robes were leaking, and I realized suddenly this was sadness I was hearing.

—They called her whore, you see. My father himself he cut off her head in the street. They took him away: it was not the modern thing to do. It did not matter. No man of our congregation would help us. And the women . . .

The face was a black shape behind the burnoose, a veiled motion, sweeping back and forth, back and forth. The day had been long: the voice and the swaying motion drew me down to sleep. I roused myself.

—What did you do?

—Do? The face turned up, and in the light from the sky the eyes glittered darkly: black pits, filmed with light. —Do? I did nothing. When a shepherd came into the city he took me back with him.

A loud spitting, a rasp of foot on shale.

—I became a shepherd. I learned a new life. I learned many things in the hills. Where the springs are. How to find the oases. And the quicksands. The season of the ewe, and the time of her bearing. I took a wife. She is a good woman. But now—

The figure leaned over, the eyes plain now in the dark face, a yard from my own. In my ear a voice was wailing.

—Now the lambs have come, and there is nothing to do. I come down to the Valley to find work. And I find you.

—What work do you do?

—I dig.

—Dig?

—Yes, dig, dig! Shovel and pick, or little brushes. Trenches this way and that. I have been a digger before. I have found many things. Valuable things. And nothing have I stolen. I have helped many digs to find.

—To find?

I was leaning forward, almost within the shadow of his robes.

He drew back, turned toward the gray band of the horizon, and shrugged.

—What they find.

The figure withdrew into his robes and a silence that enveloped us both in a circle cut off from the world. I looked up to reassure myself that the sky was still there: the roof of the world was hung with lamps shivering in the cooling night.

—What makes you think I'm here to find anything?

He spat again, but did not move.

—What do you think I'm here to find?

The figure leaned forward.

—I know you. I know your name.

I drew back as if from a snake.

—Your name is ———, you come from ——— in United States. You are a professor-doctor. I worked for you, two years ago, down there.

The arm pointed now, a short straight thrust into the Valley of the Kings, where dim slopes slanted over deeper shadows. —You found a tomb. There was a man in it. I was there when you—

—When I what?

The face was inches from mine.

—When you took the bottle. You put it there.

The finger jabbed at my breastbone.

—You put it there, and went away, exactly like a thief. And now you are here.

—Here? My voice was weak.

His voice was low, murmuring, a thick haze. —Was it a map?

Murmuring deep in my skull, a pulsing darkness speaking: —Yes.

—Of this place?

—Yes.

He mumbled something I could not catch.

—What? What about this place?

Teeth flashed, a finger held over them. —Shh. Shh. Shhhhhh.

—Sah. Breakfast is ready.

He had taken my powdered eggs, my Primus stove, and fixed for us a yellow mess that steamed, smelling of curry, from the plate he held under my nose.

—Sah. Come eat. We must work now before the sun.

I sat up tangled in my sleeping bag, trying to break free from it. Something else clung to me—a dream, a voice that murmured from the earth. Soft touches lingered about my skin.

There was light low in the east, hardening the Nile out of night. Beyond the river a suggestion of low, rugged hills.

Before the sun, he had said. Surely he could not think we would knock off work at noon? I had before me, with or without his help, weeks of bitter labor, and I would have put it off if I could. But having started I would finish it as quickly as strength would allow. I could not imagine an afternoon idling beside a pit half-dug and leading so suggestively down.

The rumbling of his voice rose behind me, a low drone like the one that had zoomed through my sleep in the night. What had I dreamed? I turned and saw him prostrate and cowled, his sandals beside him where he knelt face-down on a rug, the soles of his feet pink in the dawn, his arms stretched out to the east.

Orange light flooded the sand and rocks, brightening to white, and when I turned to the east the ragged hills were lost in glare. Halfway down the slope, a pool of shadow in a natural hollow in the scree, a pit opened. Beside it rubble was strewn down the slope, hurled as if a monstrous dog had dug there, dug all night in the frenzy of a scent, a scent that I too smelled now, on the hot breaths of dawn: dust, spice, bitumen and natron, the mummy of a god.

I shook my head. Foolishness, put there by this man's chanting.

But this hole: what was I to make of this hole? For it was a hole, not a pit or trench or any of the ordinary excavations. It was a passageway, leading down. Too big, too wide, too deep for any one man's one night's work. The shepherd's voice droned through my thoughts, distracting. Had he hypnotized me then? Had I slept weeks away? Surely I must be suggestible to anything by now.

I looked to the shepherd, who had risen from his rug, rolled it, and was now absorbed in picking pieces of egg from his beard. Haunted by the feeling of a void hovering somewhere in my memory—days taken out of my life—I walked with him to inspect his work.

The interior was dark, a meter high, perhaps—high enough to crouch in, if one bent almost double; it slanted down some fifteen meters or more, seeming to end in a flat, featureless mass.

How had he done it?

I ached to ask, but caution kept me still: if I asked, he might disappear, this fabulous passage might close, and I would awake on a barren hillside, weeks of heartbreaking labor still before me. The man crouched at my shoulder, his breath audible in my ear.

—Have you a torch, sah?

I had indeed: a six-cell indestructible pharos, bought expressly to illuminate the endless corridors of the King. By its light, the shepherd let me lead him down.

Scree tumbled beneath my feet, a cascade of stones preceding me down the tunnel. I heard them strike and lie still. In the passage, sound was magnified, my breath coming fast, panting thickly. Behind me, the shepherd padded noiselessly down, dislodging not a pebble. The light showed us the tunnel's end, a smooth, seamless face of stone.

In any other tomb, the lack of carving on the door would have sunk my spirits, made me think of turning away from one too obscure to repay the cost of opening. Here, the blankness set off a pounding in my ears, a lightness in my chest, a voice hinting: Here is a secret announcing itself.

—Sah. There is no door.

He was right. Blankness was very well, but this stone seemed a solid mass: we might be at bedrock.

—Could we widen the excavation?

My voice was a hoarse whisper, too loud.

—Sah. There is no door. You should turn back.

He clutched my hand, pulling me up. —Go home, sah. There is no passage for you here.

His hands were plucking at my fingers, at my clothes. I pushed him back.

—I have no home, you filthy—

—*Sah!*

Silence seeped like bad air down the hole, filling the space between us.

—Sah.

He was breathing heavily. His eyes were pits again. —There is something.

He brushed past me in the narrow way without touching, and I heard rock scrape rock. He passed behind me again.

—There, sah. His eyes did not turn up. —Perhaps that is what you wish.

The beam of my flashlight lit on a hemisphere of polished rock projecting from the blank surface. I fell on it, my hands curved around its cool, smooth surface. In a backward glance I saw the Arab's eyes grow wide, and then he was gone, the world was black and I was falling, a wind whispering fear in my groin.

I fell long enough to consider these: the hemisphere's swift motion at my touch; the answering motion of the rock beneath me; a momentary glimpse of the opening chute; that the Arab's mouth had opened too; that this was absurd.

Then the darkness imploded.

Let the abomination speak not my name in Neter-kert:

For my place is my own, my name and my body are my own, and all things are my own in the Duat.

For I am Khepera, the self-created, the speaker
of my name.
For mine are the Words of Power.

I clutched something to my chest, unsure what it was, knowing only that, with nothing else to hold, this must be worth
holding. My head ached, and the darkness around me whirled
and whistled until I thought the floor had given way again.
I lay amid sandy rubble; the object I held was the flashlight,
broken or switched off in the first convulsion of my fall. I sat
up, and the darkness whirled.
    I pressed the switch.

There comes a point in any excavation, if it is a successful one,
when you no longer care for the significance of your finds. The
articles you uncover, the articles you will write about them, the
reception by the profession of your work—all of these cease to
matter. What you want—all you want—is to get to the center: to unlock the sarcophagus, remove the outer coffin, and
the next, and the next—but even when you have the mummy
exposed before you, its amulets and ornaments, its most personal possessions shrinking where they protrude from the yellow linen—even this is not enough. You will not rest until you
have stripped the cere-cloths away and stared upon the face of

him for whom all this has been done, of whose life these dumb objects struggle to speak.

It is the face, finally, that you desire. And although the nose withers, and the fine leather everywhere draws back, the absent eyes turned inward as if regarding the hollow left by the embalmers, still you search it for some answer.

Something haunts the lips. After centuries of silence, as the process of desiccation stretches the slackness of death, do these lips purse, do they part again, to deliver the secret they have lingered so long on life's after threshold to tell? This is what we come for: not science, not gold. Only this: the promise of a voice that knows.

Fabulous things. A pandemonium of things. A chaos of things, and everywhere the gleam of gold, the glint of silver, sparks of ruby, amethyst, emerald receding infinitely into darkness. All of this reflected in a single slow sweep of light. So much I had expected. So much I had seen before, and I relaxed, slightly. Only slowly did the significance bear in on me of what the light did *not* show.

There were no walls.

I struggled to my feet, slashing the beam about. Light fled over inconceivable heaps of footstools, hassocks, chairs, couches, a throne with the gold head of a lion: off dimly in the distance a ship, full-rigged, oars feathered, its sail dark gossamer, motionless. All of these I saw, but no sign of an end: only an endless expanse of dull gold beneath no canopy of

utter black. At an impossible height above the floor the darkness seemed to roll, as if black clouds gathered there, but not a
breath of wind stirred my hair, although the hairs themselves
were stirring.

Had my eyes been damaged by the fall? Was this the time I
had been dreading, when the disease would eat into something
essential, and all appearance of reality would be torn finally
away? I felt my occiput for signs of damage, but no damage
could I find: for all I knew I was not hurt, and so this must, for
all I knew, be real.

I felt for something solid at my back. The blank, polished
wall down which I had fallen sloped steeply up into darkness.
For a distance of seven feet above the floor, and as many to the
right and left, no sign of a join or crack could I find. The face
of the wall was itself peculiar: of a stone polished like obsidian
and as dark, it presented to my eyes and fingertips an absolutely
smooth and seamless surface, of a temperature indistinguishable from my skin. Touching it, I could barely convince myself
that I felt substance. And something more: though polished
to a glassy smoothness, and of the most flawless ebony, it gave
back no reflection of my light, seeming to swallow up the beam
within itself. The light appeared to penetrate the thickness of
an inch or so (though a lunatic portion of my mind, which
intermittently set the blood to pounding in my ears, insisted
that the distance was far greater) before fading, as in dense
smoke. Slight security to have it at my back, as the heaps of
treasure grimaced and edged closer to me, unless I held them
back with the light (and in the light they receded endlessly,
which soon unnerved me more than their approach).

It was after this inspection of the wall, when I turned back to face again the vast cavity of dead air, that the helplessness of my situation came near to defeating me, and for a moment I was convinced that the fall had killed me, and that I must start out now on the journey of the dead, seeking the gateway to an afterlife that must, perforce, be the Egyptian one.

But my feet beneath me were unnerved; warmth had deserted me, and my breath seemed sticking in my throat. I could no more move a step into that darkness than I could— I could not think of an alternative. In the jittering beam of my light, the mountains of carved faces—eyes and open mouths—edged closer.

I picked up a rock and hurled it at them; in a shower of glittering sand the darkness swallowed it down.

The soundlessness was terrifying, a vertigo, like the horror one feels at one's own emptiness while looking over the rim of a high cliff.

If I stood much longer at this wall, I knew, the soundlessness would wash me over in a black flood, press me against—into— the black rock, where behind me dim shapes moved. I turned and saw my face, fading, and turned my light again to frieze a grinning serpent, carnelian-eyed: a ceremonial staff. I knew that if I remained here, in moments terror would strip me of whatever power of conscious action I yet possessed.

I stepped out among the burial offerings to the King.

So I thought them: burial offerings. As I walked among them, a familiar voice revived within me, commenced cataloging, dating, guessing dynasties, proveniences, and there seemed at first no qualitative difference from the tombs of ordinary mortals I had rifled. But as I walked among mounds of treasure heaped in places to five times my height, strewn so thickly that at times I must abandon the floor to clamber on shifting cracking crumbling stacks of gilded chairs, panniers of bread, unguent-cups, burnished braziers, sphinxes, anubises, amulets, maces, trumpets, candlesticks, fans, every uncountable object of inscrutable intent, I began to doubt. These were no offerings: no nation, not even Egypt, could give up its wealth so wantonly, not to bury it forever with a dead King. The entire land had been stripped.

I knew now why no trace of him remained above the ground. There had been no silence. There had been no stilling of Egypt's voice in the years of the King. It was all here. He had collected it all.

And then I knew also, with a certainty that made me gasp again in the still air of—not a tomb—I knew how wrong I had been, how utterly wrong from the start. The work of effacement, the revenge I thought his followers had wreaked on him: the silence that had swallowed him had been his own. He had set himself beneath his own horizon, then sealed shut the door, leaving no memory of himself behind. The word of power—if such there was—was a word to enforce oblivion.

So I told myself, but as I wandered through a wilderness of wealth, I knew it must have been far more than that. But what, and how, or why, still I did not know. What certainty I had once possessed was gone now, shattered by the force of my fall into—into something I could not even name: no single name seemed adequate any more. I could only walk, and, in the brief flashes I allowed myself of light, wonder.

I wandered at first through a warehouse of furniture, all made in the form of fabulous beasts.

When I turned on the light again I was neck-deep in pottery, blue glass jugs and bronzed ewers, faience flasks, bowls, vases, oviform urns.

I switched on the light again: towers of awls, adzes, augurs; saws, plumb lines, spatulas, trowels and glowing copper knives.

Out of darkness softness brushed my face, dropped down a clinging web about my head: linens, dyed in the geometries of Phoenicia, dim blue and rust.

I walked in a dry harbor of barges, feluccas lateen and square-rigged, galleys of fifty oars.

Baskets of grain, fields of wicker heaped high, receding to a dark horizon.

And in the distance, a dim reflection of my light: a wall.

I ran, scattering grain about me. I ran past endurance; stopped, small cries fluttering around me. I fed myself on fists full of grain gone soft as dust with age, and slaked my thirst from sealed jugs, smashing off their lids with unechoing blows, the liquid splashing across the floor, running under earthenware into darkness.

I ran, and drew no nearer to the light, no longer seeing what blocked my steps, familiar now with the unspeakable variety of the unfamiliar. I smashed it and ran over the remains.

I no longer ran. I stumbled, and as the time—minutes or months—passed, the wall grew higher, and lowered above me. And still it was beyond my outstretched hand.

I slept, atop pads of linen, a roll of bandage cloth beneath my head, the smell of age in my nostrils, and in my sleep a voice ran on, chanting names I did not know.

THE WALL OF the world I would have thought it, so high it climbed into what should have been the sky. To left and right my flashlight showed it vanish into darkness, as if it turned a corner into night. The wall was white, alabaster I thought from the warm, almost fleshly glow in my light. At the base of the wall, an empty cartouche, inlaid with gold, defined the outlines of a doorway. Beyond that door, the empty cartouche promised, I would find the King's own name, and take it for my own.

A glyph, in gold, was centered above the door. It was a word of command: *Uba*. Open. Was I supposed to speak? I tried to say *Uba*, but my mouth was afraid. I approached closer, hoping I would see somewhere about it a polished hemisphere of stone. Behind me the darkness grew deeper. The old, familiar chill blew through me, and I was afraid.

There was no polished stone. I shone the beam upward in a spreading cone of light. There, five or fifty meters above my head, a dim suggestion of white on white, I thought I saw a protrusion, perhaps a dome of smooth stone. Perhaps the height was an illusion, I told myself, and reached. My hand stretched out, my arm pitifully short: it reached not even to the top of the door. I let it fall upon the door then, thinking that I would pound an answer from beyond, although I knew no one would answer.

My hand fell, but the door was not there: my arm swung an arc through empty air.

I was dizzy with the illusion, and almost fell into what I now saw plainly as an open archway. The space beyond was a tunnel, leading sharply down, its interior formed of the same blank white stone. The milky substance held no shadow, annihilating perspective: it was *uba*—open—; what I had read as a command had been a description.

Steep stairs descended to a lower level, a low passageway through which I was forced to move on all fours. I hesitated, uneasy at the thought of all that darkness at my back.

I crouched low and crawled, the torch in my mouth.

A strange smell permeated the corridor: familiar, but alarmingly unplaceable. It raised gooseflesh on me before I had gone a dozen yards into the corridor.

The tunnel gave out high in the wall of the room that breathed the smell, and as my head emerged in open air I knew it, and was afraid again. The smell was *damp*: never in my life had I smelt water in an Egyptian tomb, where it could only mean something horribly amiss, indistinguishable from the fetor of death. But smelling it here, so strongly that my face seemed drenched in it, unnerved me for another reason as well, and more than anything I had seen in the great hall. The myriads of artifacts gathered there, the size of the construction—those had been mere logistics and engineering. But maintaining water in a tomb for over four thousand years: this was magic. This was something terrible, beyond my compass, a mystery of life-in-death.

From my perch high in the wall I shone the light around the cavern. At one time I might have thought it large: twenty meters, perhaps, in its longest dimension. Now it seemed uncomfortably cramped. Featureless, but for the water that filled it to a height perhaps a dozen feet below my downturned face. Only reluctantly did I shine the light down on the still surface (a mirror of obsidian, I might have thought it, were the smell of it not sending damp fingers over my flesh), and with an unreasoning horror of what I might see in its depths.

I saw only a bright disc of light. A disc of deeper darkness floated at its side. Between the reflection of the flashlight and the darkness in my eyes I saw only my own face, a dim-lit ovoid pale upon the water.

There was no ledge around the chamber; the floor was given over entirely to the pool, nor were there steps or rungs or cleats of any sort leading from my perch down to the surface. A dozen feet or so: not much to dive. And if the water is only inches deep? I will suffer a slight fall, nothing worse, I told myself. And if it is deep? I will swim. But neither falling nor drowning held me there, despite the terror I felt gathering in the constricted darkness at my back. The water itself: it frightened me. What might be in water that old? What slime? What smells? What— Before the panic could take me, I took one breath and swung out into the center of the pool.

I have no way of knowing how deep the water was: only that I fell; the water struck cold into my groin, and then closed over my head. My eyes were shut tight. I sank, and while my pulse was loud in my ears the water swirled about me and, disoriented, I imagined that I continued to descend. Then my hand broke into air, a scum at the surface clinging as if I had pierced a membrane, and my head was free and I could breathe. I trod water, hearing a whimpering in the darkness, magnified against the lowering roof. I lifted the hand that held the flashlight, fumbled for the switch, terrified lest it should slip from my hands and I be lost forever in the dark, unable to find any exit from this pool.

I swept the beam around, and no sign of an opening could I find. I berated myself: I had known of pits in passageways, knew why they were placed, yet more credulous than any ignorant grave-robber I had flung myself in this one. I was treading water much too energetically: the voice in me remarked that I would be exhausted in a minute, but I did not care. In a series of leaps, I flung myself half into the air, the awful water closing viscous over my head each time I fell back down, filling my mouth and nose with a taste of black brackishness.

I swam to one end of the pool, and found there only slick stone, repulsive to touch. I swam toward the other end, and abruptly my feet found something solid. I was afraid of it, but my arms were lead, and my legs were lead, and my chest was a stone dragging me down. I stood, and the thing in the water did not move.

The water shelved toward the far end; the walls converged, the ceiling lowered, and there, in an angle of the room, I found six steps that took me to a door.

A real door: no trickery here. But what a door: silver doorposts (their name is *ah-ti*, I told myself), golden panels (*at, ati-t,* I called them) burnished to a skin-like finish; and the panels were inlaid in tourmaline, sodalite, carnelian and jasper, the gems agleam in the light of my torch, all inlaid in the form of Horus-eyes. *Beka-ti*, the voice within me whispered. *Beka-ti: beg, begg, beg-t, bagaau.* The eyes gleamed as if moist.

Before I could touch it the door buckled, one hinge breaking away from the doorpost: the sound of its fall boomed loudly around me.

I started back, wavering over the water. A ripple ran through the pool, out, then back, then out again.

The door hung askew now. Wary without knowing why, I kicked at it: the lower hinge twisted, tore free, and the door crashed inward, sending out a cloud of dust. I coughed, the smell of it filling my nostrils, thick on my tongue. I spat it out at once.

No one who has worked with them can forget the smell of mummy. The door seemed to have fallen onto one, possibly several of them, breaking them to bits. I shone the flashlight through the opening. The door lay across half a dozen shrouded forms, stuffed within the chamber apparently without ceremony. The wrappings were plain, the workmanship of the lowest quality. I wondered what I had stumbled into, and turned the beam about the room.

Mummies. Mummies everywhere.

Piles of them, arms clenched tightly at their breasts, linen wrappings dissolving, falling away into cobwebs: leather and sticks protruding, and here and there the bright gleam of tooth.

The proportions of the chamber were odd. The flashlight shining over the banks of dead, the perspective seemed strangely askew. I could only tell, from the numbers of the dead I saw, and the vague masses extending beyond the limit of the beam, that the space was large. But the dimensions of the chamber were not so great as those of the hall above. The beam of the torch fell finally on a wall, far distant beyond stacks of brown. Once I had found the limits of the vault, I could guess the number of dead piled here, and another of the mysteries of the King was plain to me. I had wondered about the workers, the tens of thousands of mutes employed in the construction of the tomb. They had disappeared from the accounts. I had found them.

Ushabti? Or the kind of men who tell no tales? Or was there something else about this display of—I could only call it wealth. The corpses were stacked, scattered about in utter disregard for funeral rites, but they were here, they had been embalmed at who could guess what expense. There was something more intended than mass murder, more than the convenient disposal of inconvenient labor.

The far wall looked very far away. Behind me the water still sloshed, and I realized now what the taste in it had been.

I soon found why the proportions of the chamber had seemed so odd: the roof sloped, or the floor rose, and before I had gone a dozen meters I was forced to proceed upon my hands and knees.

There was another chamber, a small room that held only a smell, a small smell, but it made me vomit until I thought my viscera would come up.

And another chamber that held only a portrait, in some kind of pigment, on the long side wall.

I had never seen its like. Done in profile, it was of a woman, somewhat between youth and middle age, looking sidelong into the room. Looking at me, recognizing me, knowing me and my purpose there, regarding all with an expression poised at the moment when amusement turns toward contempt or grief or fear. There was that about her I cannot explain, only that it made me weep again, with an anguish I thought could never abate.

I faced another door. On it the familiar, empty cartouche. It stood half-open onto darkness. I pressed it, and it swung, soundlessly, as frictionless as dream. Beyond I could see nothing, only the infinitely deeper darkness that I carried with me: it pulsed in the center of the floor.

The portrait smiled down on me as I entered the room.

A very barren room. A very dead end. A blank wall curving away to the left of me, another away to the right. And on the far side, where the walls recurved and met, completing a circle, I saw what I had come to find: a royal cartouche.

It was empty.

I barely looked back as the door swung to behind me, nor cared when I heard something snap at its close. I only stood, and stared, knowing that I had reached my destination, and there was nothing here.

I could not accept it. I could not believe it. I could only think that there was some trick here, some secret I was missing, something I had overlooked. Perhaps the glyphs were there, shallowly graven, and in the pallid alabaster my flashlight failed to shadow them. I moved cautiously to my left, hoping that the oblique rays of light would shade a shallow relief; I circled around the room, tethered to the empty cartouche by my flashlight's beam, by my own gaze that would not let the emptiness go, by the dark circle that pulsed there—now pulsing harder, now almost audible in the extraordinarily silent air. I edged to my left, circling, but the wall remained a blank. When I stood before the cartouche and ran my fingers over its cool, indifferent surface, I felt nothing.

Only then did the enormity of the thing bear in on me at last. It was a trap. As though laid down long ago for me and me alone, through five millennia it had led me, across the continents and decades of my own life, to this empty ending. And I, driven by a need I had not stopped to question, a credulity that even now makes me grimace in the darkness with embarrassment, though there is no one here to see—freighted with all this burden of desire and dread, I had come. I had answered the call. I am here.

Unconsciously, I had started to back away from the blank cartouche, as though I suspected in it some power to ensnare me still, to wind me deeper in extremities of self-love and self-deceit. I backed away. My feet scraped sound from the floor, cutting through the silence that had swathed my thoughts numb, letting in flashes of fact: the certainty that the door behind me had locked; the conviction that I would find in it

no mechanism of release; the faint but definite indications
that my flashlight was failing; all the long distance at my back,
of corridor and chamber, unscalable wall and empty sky; and
beyond that sky, over the ocean my life in ruins behind me; and
before me a darkness pulsing, deeper, blacker, until the real
darkness closing in seemed only the ashen shadow of despair.
My heart stood on my shoulder, shouting. Against the darkness I saw, repeated in flashes that came to me with the vivid
immediacy of lightning, the leathery stare of horror in the face
of Nur-Mar's Answerer; I remembered how we had found
him crouched, head furled close to his drawn-up knees: I felt
the same urge tightening in my chest, struggling to curl itself
around the void left by my soul.

I do not know—and even now some fugitive spirit of curiosity will not let the question alone—just what it was that made
me stop. Perhaps it was the panic seizing me at last. Perhaps
it was despair. But I suspect, rather, it was the perverse spirit
that has led me so infallibly to this place. It had not finished
with me yet. I was to be its toy some hours more. Whatever
it was, it prevented me from taking the final step backward,
which would (I think of it now with regret) have been my last.
It would have been much easier to tumble in blindly backward,
not knowing until too late just what my feet had done.

Air breathed up the back of my neck. The hairs there
stirred. A smell—not damp, not dry, but infinitely corrupt—
penetrated finally through my terror. Some sense for which I
have no name registered emptiness behind me. As if in a dream,
or acting out in waking life a dream I had long ago forgotten,
I turned, knowing already just what I would find: a pit some

ten feet across and immeasurably deep occupied the center of the room. In the same uncanny doubleness I teetered, caught in the centripetal pull of the pit but unable, finally, to allow myself to fall.

I fell back instead to lie in darkness. Ghostly chuckling echoed upward from the mortar my foot had dislodged, loosening more echoes from the depths of the well. I heard no impact.

I lay for a long time before lighting the torch again. The ceiling was low, and marked, above the center of the well, with a small gathering of glyphs: *Akha*, it read: enter, go. But when I looked more closely, I saw that the word was incomplete: the last sign of the glyph was broken. Either the engraving was shaved plane, or the stone had fallen into the well, but I knew, as plainly as if it had been spoken aloud, as if I had always expected to find it here, what the entire glyph would be. *Akha-t*, the glyph had said, still echoing over the empty centuries the pride and despair of a King, and a cynicism deeper still. The glyph gestured to the well at my feet, embracing as well the immense edifice around me, the King's death, my own life, and all the world of light that I had lost long, long ago: *Akha-t*: a disease of the womb.

I had found what Khafre's Sphinx was still seeking in the sky over Giza: the answer opened at my feet.

There was little else to do. I knew better than to try the door, although I did. I knew better than to search the walls and ceiling, to pry at the joints between the stones, but I did. I did these things, and several others, until my own bloody finger-prints marked the room. Time passed. The air in the room grew foul, and not all of the foulness came from the well. The flashlight, no matter now I saved it, grew dim. I was hungry, light-headed, and the voice in my ears was loud.

Only one discovery did I make in these hours in my tomb, one last contribution I have to make to human knowledge. Forgive me: the dreadful cynicism of the King's last gesture is infecting me at last—or my own despair has finally unleashed itself, now that there is no shred of human society left to hold it back. But if I am bitter, it is not without reason. He did not leave me even so much of my pride as this: even this, my last discovery, was determined long ago, this neat stack of papyrus placed here at the margins of the floor where, sooner or later, I must stumble over it.

And obey.

As though they held some potent spell, once I found the sheets of paper I had no choice: Ser, Serr, Ser metut: arrange words in order, compose a work: write. Of course the papyrus crumbled through my fingers: dust, swirling in the last rays of my flashlight. I thought at first that this too was another piece in the puzzle, another refinement of a torture I could hardly understand: to be commanded to write, and given only dust. Almost I rebelled again: I shoveled the ashes down the chute. But when I found the pens, purest ivory, still supple and sharp, bound with a linen cord beside their alabaster ink-pot, the powdered ink waiting in its stoppered flask, I gave myself up at last to the command. I sat, I crossed my legs in the old, familiar posture of the scribe, and *ari metchut*: I made a book.

The fluid for the ink I supplied in the only way I could. My pockets I emptied for what small evidences of my past they could provide: my journal notebook, scraps of letters, old index cards. Words came to me out of the darkness. And although I cannot see what I write, these words will suffice. They will survive me, I know, just as the King's monument survived him: as long as time requires, and the darkness in the pit endures.

Out of that darkness, reader, I reach my hand to you.

SCYLLA

ἐρέω δέ τοι ἀμφοτέρωθεν
—ODYSSEY XII:58

It was a fair cruise, the seas calm, the winds and currents favoring, the skies so clear the evening star was visible by day. Mornings and evenings low clouds rolled, pink in the sunrise, orange in the west; always they vanished before us. The crew, off watch, hung in the shrouds, where they swung with the long surge of the sea; high in the foretop, Teofilo, the Portygee, sang in his languid tongue. This was in the days before the Law.

On the fortieth day we spoke a ship, heavy-laden out of the east. Its captain told us that the Law had come.

"What is the Law?" I called back, but the ship had drifted out of hailing. It settled over the horizon, and we never saw it again. On the sixtieth day, we spoke a black, lean ship, an eye painted on its prow. Its captain howled at us like a madman, and evidently he was mad, for his crew had tied him to the mast, and rowed as though the devil was after them. We pulled away on a freshening wind.

On the ninetieth day, in calm seas we spoke a monstrous vessel, all iron and smoke among the ice. It told us, too, the Law had come, but when we asked what this Law might be it only forged ahead, full speed into the night. And on the last day of our voyage, as the lighthouse top rose out of the west, and then the steeple on the hill, and we made our way into the harbor, clear and smooth as glass, the shadow of the moon ghosted across our wake, a shudder shook our canvas as if the wind had died, and a hollow voice from astern told us that the Law had come.

We stepped ashore, all uncertain of what this Law might be, and what it might mean to us, men returned from a long voyage on the sea.

At first, it seemed nothing had changed. The inn at the wharf was lighted as ever, the fire still burned on its hearth, the smoke still smudged against the low roll of cloud as it always had, and the landlord welcomed us as he always had. Our gear piled in the corner smelled strongly of the sea, and that, too, was as it always had been, the salt smell suddenly strange among the smells of earth.

And on the next morning, as we rose from the arms of our sweethearts and wives, this, too, was as it had always been. And we asked them, I asked my wife, what this was about the Law. And then there was a change. Her eyes clouded, as though struggling to remember. Her hands smoothed absently a corner of the counterpane, as though in it she sought to read this Law.

"Is it nothing then?" I prompted her. "Is it only a yarn?"

"No," she said, slow and uncertain, bewildered at her inability to remember. "No, it is not that." But what the Law might be she could not recall, and I could not guess.

My crew had all dispersed. I caught the last of them, the bosun, as he waited by the depot, shortly after noon. When I questioned him, he told me that the crew had all gone home.

"Gone home?" I said to him. "Their homes are here—what homes they have. And what business have sailors to talk of home ashore? At sea, we talk of home. But ashore, we talk of the sea. That is how it has always been."

"I know," said the bosun, fingering a lanyard woven 'round his neck. "But that was before the Law." His fingers traced the length of the lanyard as if it irritated the skin beneath his chin. I noticed suddenly his beard was gone. His fingers reached the lanyard's end, and missed the whistle that had hung there.

I collared him. "Back to the ship, me hearty," I cried, but even I could tell my heart was no longer in it: the boisterous tones fell flat in the dusty street.

"Please, Captain." The bosun's eyes were pleading, more for me than for himself. In the street around us, people were staring. In the sunstruck street my sou'wester shone a ridiculous yellow.

In the harbor I found the ship had gone.

AND SO THIS was what the Law must be, I told myself, and felt already the strength of its claim on me. I felt it in the easy acquiescence to the loss of my ship, a ship I had not even had the chance to go down with. At low tide, I prowled the breakwater, but not a mast stuck out above the glassy harbor. A flock of pigeons broke from the steeple, wheeled once above the seaward channel, and I knew then that my ship had gone that way, and I remembered suddenly that none of us, in our eagerness for shore, had bothered to secure her. She had simply drifted out to sea. And this, I knew, must be the Law as well—not the tide, but our forgetting of our duty.

Our old duty, I should say. Keeping watch. Standing to the wheel. Going aloft in all weathers, even when the ice stood so sharp upon the shrouds that our hands bled. I speak, of course, for the crew. And the lookout who had never failed us, never failed in the sight of land, the sight of other shipping, of curiosities—whales, uncharted islands—of the sea: how had he failed to warn us of the Law? How had I failed to steer us clear?

And now I find new duties, here upon the land. I am not captain, of course. I work now among other men, my sou'wester on the shelf of the hall closet in our home. It is a snug home. My wife has tried to keep it as much as possible like a ship, and for this I am grateful, but I find, as the weeks go on, the neighbors' curiosity makes me self-conscious. I may replace the portholes with proper windows soon, before the winter comes. It will be better to have the light.

And I correspond, of course, with my old crew. This, too, I think, is something of the Law: they wrote, sending in their new addresses. Teofilo, the Portygee, writes from Providence, where he works in dry goods; Sundays he still sings, in a choir. My first mate, in Hartford, has taken up the insurance trade. The cook, of course, is unemployed, but hopeful.

And so they all wrote in. Some sent snapshots of their children, grown astonishingly over the course of our last voyage. Already there are college plans, small triumphs of the rising generation, and already there are sorrows. A collection for Anderson, whose youngest died of fever, makes the rounds. This too, I know, is of the Law.

But what this Law is, and who decreed it, still I do not know. I work all day in city hall, a petty functionary recording deeds, and you would think that here, surrounded by machineries of regulation, recording, order, here the agencies of Law would show themselves. But it is not so simple, and I think this complexity as well, it too is of the Law.

I have made my own investigations. I have collared them in the marmoreal halls of the county courthouse, back there across the parking lot, beside the jail, from which occasionally angry voices rise, occasionally a tattooed hand reaches forth, and once already I have known the tattoo, remembered it when it had pulled upon an oar, and felt the profoundest pity seeing it now, livid on an arm grown pale in confinement, the hand that once pulled yare now a helpless fluttering upon a window-pane. I have buttonholed them, I say, between meetings, trying to ascertain who might be the Law, who might know what clause in it decreed the drifting of my ship.

Here, too, the Law intercedes. I feel it dividing me, cluttering my speech with doubts, with qualifications. Where once I might have roared, "Avast! I'll split ye, ye beggars," and all manner of stout nonsense, now I find myself not wanting to press too urgently, not wanting to reveal my ignorance of the Law, but wondering as well, as this city councilman I grip seeks this way and that around me, his eyes rolling like a whale in its flurry as he looks for someone to rescue him: I have wondered if he knows, it anyone knows, just what is going on. I wonder if these lubbers, who were once so content to feed us, drunk us, bed us down and ship us out, to take our cargo, our fish, our rendered blubber and our ambergris, I wonder if they are so content now as they seem, under their Law.

For I cannot but feel it is their Law. I tell myself, angry even as I worry if I go too far with this collared councilman, that this was none of my doing, and then I feel the doubt, I wonder if this Law were not some stowaway on my own ship, a rat that slunk down the first hawser carrying the Law within its fur, but then I tell myself that doubts such as these are just the workings of the Law, a teredo worm upon the stout oak of my heart, but it is too late, the councilman has escaped, in tow with two county attorneys. They depart, promising to meet over lunch next week when I have written up a brief, and I am left holding a starched paper collar in my hands, and no closer to knowing how I might regain my ship.

And this, I know, is not the Law: I want my ship again. I dream of it in the night, dream that I have awakened, thrown back the curtains in the moonlight, flung up the sash, and there, from the second storey of my snug home, which still looks down upon the harbor, the harbor still smooth as glass, there in the moonlight my ship glides in past the breakwater, there on the wharf my crew are all assembled, the townspeople as of old, wives and sweethearts, innkeepers and merchants all waving, all sobbing, all joyous to see us off, and we are joyous, stout, absorbed in our work, running up and down the rat-lines, departing on the tide. And there at the channel's end, as a favoring wind freshens at our stern, our wake begins to boil, the harbormaster's boat frets against the side, and the pilot, climbing overboard, reaches up to shake my hand. His grip is strong, it pulls me after, and together we fall into no harbormaster's boat, only into water deep, and cold, and I awake, I have thrown the counterpane aside and lie shivering in a sweat that has cooled upon my skin, chill now in the breeze from the open window, the window which, as I rise to close it, I see looks down on no harbor, but only into my neighbor's yard. On his roof a windvane in the shape of a whale swings, moodily complaining to the moon. This too I recognize as the workings of the Law.

I have learned to recognize it. It is clearest in the shape of the hills off to the west, the notch in them where the sun, on these December evenings, sets. They were not there, those hills, when we left on our last voyage. But it is not in their existence that I trace the Law in its clearest function—not in the fact of them so much as in their action. The way they catch at the eye, the way they block the horizon that once lay so vividly flat there was no mistaking that the world was round, the sun a mighty vessel gone hull-down on the horizon, and the whole globe an ocean. Now, these hills, they give a weight, an unfair advantage, to the land, and even the sun seems to sink beneath it. In this I see most clearly the workings of the Law: in this, and in the way I have taken to staring westward, the sea at my back almost always now, almost as if I have forgotten it is there, I look away from it, I look landward, where my crew has gone, and wonder when I will follow them.

I know the stories. Certainly I know the traditions, the gear

I should carry, the questions I should wait for. When I should plant the oar. If I am lucky, if the land be fertile, perhaps the oar will sprout. God knows, any oar I find in this town will be green enough.

But I resist, divided in myself, and feeling in that division the workings of the Law. The fluorescent lights in my office, the soft muttering of the television set at home, the children who each day astonish me as they grow strange and stranger, their voices roughen, their faces lengthen, until I seem to have come home to the wrong house by mistake, and somewhere down this line of cottages my life is waiting, my wife wondering what can be keeping me: all of this, I know, is the Law.

Only, I tell myself, only this questioning, only my doubt that these changeling children can be my own, only my conviction that my life lies elsewhere, in the dream of my ship's return: only here, I tell myself, and in this story I tell you, hoping you will understand—only here I hold the Law at bay.

But it is hard. I feel the weakening of my resolve, the strength of my limbs draining away under the Law. I have, in fact, grown old here on the land. Each year at Christmastide, the cards are fewer. Anderson died last year, succumbing to the curse that seems to have dogged his family, a curse we all know to be the workings of the Law, but why it should have worked more strongly in him than in the others, I do not know. The years have passed as quickly as any dream, the children are truly strangers, voices on the telephone. There are resentments between us now, old grudges I cannot remember, and these, too, are the workings of the Law.

Only my wife resists; only in her do I feel as if time and

the Law might have their exceptions. Our bodies, of course, it owns entire. They luff in a failing wind. We blow as we climb the hill to our home, and the second floor is shut off, cold in the winters, an odd, faint, salt smell there, as if in some forgotten closet my old sea-gear lies moldering. Every thing about us succumbs to the Law, except in certain moments, rare always but constant, moments, perhaps, when she walks me to the wharf, and places me so as to look out to the sea, knowing (I have complained of it) that I forget, and stands beside me in a companionable silence. In these moments, I notice that her eyes have not changed, not in all the years that have vanished under the Law. And though the pressure of her hand upon my arm is uncertain now, the shiver in it always there, the fingertips cold often of late, something there, as well, I feel has not changed.

But is this enough? When the Law comes finally at last to claim us, what then?

For I know this as well about the Law: It is inscrutable in its workings, irrational and slow. It will not take us together, nor will it take us quickly. Not often these days, not like in the early days, when an ax upon a scaffold, a scything of plague, or even shipwrecks that I read of in the news: these, it seems, are things of the past. It will be more decorous, more closely regulated, until, at last, even our breathing will come under its control. When that moment is here, and we are finally sunk beneath the Law, I doubt that even the color of her eyes will be the same to me.

My crew have not responded to my letters; the telephone rings and rings in empty rooms. A few who linger here along the seashore tell me they are old now, the sea is no life for them. Only my wife and I still watch, and we are feeble, but still she helps me look toward the sea. We have been talking. At nights, when I cozen myself in thinking that the Law is asleep, we speak low together beneath the counterpane of what still might be. Tomorrow, I tell her, the winds may have changed, the currents may have brought her back again around the globe. Tomorrow she may ride there at the wharf, and we might board her. It could be done. They have done amazing things with ship's tackle now: the two of us might manage her alone. And my wife, companionable, agrees, and plans what ports we might call on, what cargoes we might carry, what distant shores we might explore.

It may be, I tell her, that the ship will founder. She may be, in a storm, too much for us, even if we fit her with the finest. It may be that those ports I used to visit all are closed now, and the shores I watched through spyglass in my youth, all jungle and desire, are settled now, are ports themselves, and under their own Law. It may be that the Law rules even over the ocean now, and that nowhere between the poles will see us free. It may be that the Maelstrom has been silenced, and the tides of Fundy channeled to the mill. All of this may be, but will you still set sail?

She nods, warm, a gentle shiver coursing through the two of us, as if the bed itself has felt the turning of the tide. At the window, a breeze blows back the curtain. Gentle moonlight washes in. And from my window, high up in the second storey, down on the glassy harbor I see our ship is riding in.

APOCALYPSE

Thou canst understand, therefore, that all our knowledge will be dead from the moment the door of the future is closed. —INFERNO X:106–108 (JOHN D. SINCLAIR, TRANSLATOR)

In the gorge the echoes faded. I found myself listening, hoping there would be no voices. For a minute or so—it may have been ten—we waited. I could hear the kitchen clock tick.

When the silence in the room became intolerable, we both stood to go.

The slate steps down into the gorge were buried in snow, and we stepped carefully, taking turns. The cold dimmed our flashlights, leaving us only the light of the sky to tell wet slate from ice. When we reached the bottom and walked out onto the frozen stream, the light lay pale around us. Tonight's wreck had joined the others without a sign. There was no fire. Through the sound of water under ice, we listened, and heard nothing.

I could feel Ellen shiver. She told me once, after we had climbed back home, that she is afraid to let me come down here alone. She worries that another car will fall. As I put an arm around her—tried to, but in our parkas the gesture turned into a clumsy shove—I looked up to the rim of the gorge, where our house stands. There the road turns sharply down toward the bridge, and the safety barrier has long since broken down.

It was a mistake to look. No cars (the night was soundless): only the hard angles of the rocks, and the bare trees threading the sky. The night was bitter cold, clear and moonless. Before, a night like this would have burned with stars, and the sky seemed infinitely far away. This night, I saw four, six, seven stars swimming, awash in a faintly luminous haze that lowers, night by night.

Ell caught me staring and pulled at my arm. She dragged us stumbling over rocks hidden in the snow to where the new wreck lay, broken-backed on the streamside. Its engine had spilled out in a single piece, hissing into the ice. Glass glittered everywhere. We bent to a place where a window had been. Inside were six bodies, all fallen on their heads. Their arms were tangled, as if still gesturing.

LAST NIGHT WAS Sunday. I had lost track of the day until, as we were halfway up the stairs, Ell asked if I had remembered to wind the clock. She has asked me this every Sunday night for seven years. It used to irritate me.

It is an heirloom, the clock. It was my father's, and his father's, and the story goes that it has been around the world ten times: a great, gleaming ship's chronometer. When I was young, my father would—rarely—consent to show me its works. I would dream about them, sometimes, in the conscious dreams that come before sleep. The gleam and the motion, the oddly susurrant ticking, merged with my pulse and my own breathing to whirr me into sleep.

At an early age I conceived the notion that the clock was responsible for time. I remain superstitious about keeping it wound, and have never let it stop since the day I inherited it, still ticking. When I opened its back that first day, I was surprised how my memory had magnified its works: the springs and cogs occupy no more than a quarter of the massive, largely empty casing. I use it to hide spare keys. Last night, when Ellen asked if I had remembered to wind the clock, I stopped on the stairs, and without a word turned back down. I felt her eyes on my back, and felt ashamed at my own carelessness.

IN LIFE I was the editor of a small science quarterly. I read widely in the literature, and so for ten years or more I was forewarned. But some part of me always believed that the world written up in the journals was imaginary. It never touched me: there were no people in it. It was an elegant entertainment, nothing more. This world—the one we live in—was real, and there could be no connection.

Can I understand what is happening? No, nor can I imagine the hour that launched it, some sixty thousand years ago, from the heart of the Milky Way. I can only tell myself facts: since I began this paragraph, it has moved two million miles closer.

The words clatter emptily about the page. I know only that when it emerged last June—a faint gleam, low in the summer sky—the world changed.

Part of me feels certain this cannot be, that all of us are in a dream, a mass psychosis: the second week of January will come after all, and we will waken, grinning at ourselves. The other part of me feels the emptiness in those words.

THERE IS A quiet over the land. We drive often now—gasoline is plentiful once more—in the hills outside the town, past farmsteads that could have been abandoned last week, or ten years ago. The livestock have broken down their fences. Cattle, horses, pigs stand in the road, root in the ditches. I saw a goat standing on a porch, forefeet up in a swing-chair, staring abstractedly into the distance. I wonder where the owners of the animals have gone, if anyone still feeds or waters them. I worry for them, should the snow lie deep this winter, and the ponds ice over.

We stop at the grocery store, and the quiet has penetrated there, too, a chill emitted from the frozen foods, the dearth of certain products. The aisles are quiet, but there is no serenity in this place. Out in the countryside there could be something like serenity. I think when I am out there that my intrusion has shattered the peace, this edginess I feel will depart with me, and the pigs will lie down again in the road and sleep. Here in the supermarket, every selection asks us: This large? How long? For what?

The pet food aisle is empty. A man had hysterics there this

week; we could hear him across the store. Everyone looked up, checked his neighbor, and looked down again.

When we found him, he was standing sobbing by his cart, his face gleaming in the fluorescent lights. I wanted to make him stop.

When I laid a hand on his shoulder, he wheeled.

—Do you have any?

I offered a package of cheese.

—No. He sleeved his nose. —Do you have any *cats*?

I tried to move him toward the dairy aisle, but he shrugged my hand away.

—It's not *fair*, he howled. —She's just a *cat*.

The last word made him blubber again. At the end of the aisle I saw Ell, looking diminished, mute—one of the frieze of strangers gathered there. I could not meet her eye.

Suddenly furious at him, I dragged him away, wanting to slap him into silence. Instead I pushed his cart across the back of the store, where he lapsed into a sullen calm. I pulled from the shelves anything I thought a cat might eat: marinated herring, heavy cream, Camembert. With each, I gestured, as if to say, —She'll like this; there, that's my favorite; isn't this good? Until his flat stare unstrung me, and I led him to the checkout.

I HAD BEEN down to the bridge, watching the sun go down across the valley. The lake is icing early this winter; the town was sunk in blue shadow. Below me, the gorge was already dark.

The deck of the bridge is an open steel grid. I hate to look down through it: the trees, foreshortened, look like bushes. I came home and found Ellen gone.

I thought at once of the gorge. In the darkening hall I stood and listened to the kitchen clock, and wondered how long I could wait before going to see. Then the door behind me opened, and she entered, swathed in her old, over-large winter coat. She looked as if she had walked in from an earlier year. She looked so familiar—and everything familiar now looks strange—I could not catch my breath and only nodded. —The roads are getting terrible, she said, bearing down drolly on the last word, balancing on one leg as she took off her boots. When she caught the expression on my face, she laughed. —Were you worrying about me?

MY APPETITE DIMINISHES each day, as I wake before dawn and pad about the house, too restless to start writing. The time required to toast a slice of bread seems too long. Were it not for Ell, I would no longer cook at all. I am wasting, I know: my face in the mirror shows its bones clearly now in the morning light. But Ellen grows. She eats with an appetite she never had before, and seems taller, broader of hip, and of shoulder and breast as well. It suits her. Her face retains its graceful lines, and somehow her cheeks are still indented beneath the high, Slavic bones. Her eyes, too, are still hooded, guarded above the strong, straight bar of her nose.

She has stopped wearing her glasses. She focuses as best she can on the empty air above her lap. What does she see? I have not asked. I watch her, and try to guess. Sometimes she looks up—suddenly, as if she has seen something marvelous—her mouth opens, and I catch my breath.

THE TELEPHONE SYSTEM still works. I hear a tone when I lift the receiver. It sounds mournful now, this fabulously complex network reduced to carrying this message of no message, this signal that says only: Ready to send. Our phone has not rung in weeks, nor is there anyone I call: I cannot imagine what there is to say. Some numbers I try no longer respond: the weather, dial-a-joke, dial-a-prayer. The number for the time survives, telling the ten-second intervals in its precise, weary voice.

Tonight I was alone in the kitchen, washing dishes. Something was rotting in the trash. For a long time I failed to recognize the smell (my sinuses are bad this winter), or even that I was smelling anything at all. Something was wrong. What had I done? I worked faster, scrubbed harder, but the feeling grew. What had I done? When I finally recognized the smell, my guilt and anxiety changed abruptly into anger. It had been Ellen's turn to take out the trash. I was certain of it.

When I found her, she was in the small upstairs room that still smells faintly of the coat of paint we gave it in the summer. She was sewing again; the light was bad. She looked up as I entered, her glasses on the table beside her, straining to focus on what I knew she could see only as the pale blur of my face. Her eyes still struggle to see at a distance; the effort gives her the look of a worried child. It is the expression that gazes out of the few early snapshots she still has. That look stopped me in the doorway. I tried to slow my breathing, hoping that, without her glasses, she had not seen the expression on my face. I pretended my grimace was a smile, walked over to her, and turned on the lamp. She smiled back and returned to her work, presenting me the part of her hair. I stooped, kissed it, and quickly left.

Out in the cold, the smell from the trash was thinner, almost fragile among the smells of wood smoke and snow as I walked past our stuffed and sealed garbage cans, through the hedge to the neighbors' drive. Their house has been dark three weeks. They left their car, which I use as a temporary dump. I would use their house, if I could bring myself to try the door. Their car is starting to fill, and even in the cold stinks dangerously, but it will be enough.

WE FOUGHT THE next morning instead. I had thrown something away—a magazine, the last number of a subscription that expired in November—before she had finished with it. She complained, I snapped, she turned and left the room. The fight continued as a mutual silence that went on throughout the afternoon. When I could no longer bear the rising tension, I brought her a cup of tea. She was reading in the upstairs room—the light was bad again—and when I set the tea beside her, she did not look up.

As I turned to leave, she cleared her throat. —I was afraid you were going to go through the trash.

I turned, and she was smiling at me over the brim of the cup. —I wouldn't have wanted it, you know. It would have stunk. Her smile broadened as she spoke, but before she could sip the tea, she was crying. I tried to comfort her, and felt ineffectual as I always do, at a loss for words. I patted her back, and wondered at the empty sound.

THE SAME DREAM has come to me these three nights. It starts in a scene I cannot forget, two faces I still see when I close my eyes. They were the first to fall into the gorge. We found them at first light, the car absurd among the boulders. The twin stars in the windshield told us what we would find inside. Perhaps it was the shock of finding them still so young, so peaceful behind the shattered glass, that reverberates now in my dreams; they looked asleep, their faces almost touching.

In my dream they wake, they speak to us, and as they tell us their story, weep—whether for each other or for us I cannot say. As they speak, their words live, showing us their last moments: the guardrail flying away, the slow, looming tilt of the far wall, and then the rocks uprushing. On the seat beside me, Ellen hovers at the corner of my eye. There is something I must tell her, but before I can speak, there is a noise, and then silence, which continues for a long time.

Ell wakes me. —You were crying.

Sitting up in the cold room, by the pale light the curtains cannot cover entirely, I turn and tell her the words the dream would not let me say. But as I speak, Ellen grows smaller, the room lengthens, the distance between us grows and still she lies only just beyond the farthest stretch of my arm. My voice makes no sound. Her lips move. Each object in the room is isolated, meaningless, and I think, This is the end, it has hap-

pened, and Ell diminishes still farther, contracting to one clear
point in the deepening gloom.

When I finally awake, the world is still, and Ellen still
beside me.

Her face relaxes every night, so that by morning the angles
and the lines have vanished, her nose is round and freckled,
and her lips are parted. Every morning the urge to clutch her,
shake her awake, almost overpowers me. I want to ask her
something—just what, I still can't say. But this morning, as
every morning, I let her sleep. The aching in my chest ebbs
slowly, and the daylight grows around us.

AT THE NEIGHBORS' back door I looked in the curtained window: dishes in the sink, a dinner for four spread on the table.
One of the chairs lay on its back, legs up in an expression of
helpless surprise. The door swung open as I pressed, and a burst
of hot, fetid air swept past me. Dinner had spoiled, filling the
kitchen with a high, wild sweetness. The room was so hot the
air seemed gelid: sweat burst out on my face. From the base-
ment I heard the furnace roar. To leave in the middle of dinner
seemed unremarkable; but why turn up the heat? I stopped
amid the ruins of the meal, stooped, and righted the chair. As I
bent, I saw in the far doorway another leg stretched out on the
floor, and beyond it a room where nothing was right.

I am afraid I understood. I could deduce—I could not stop
myself from observing—the tools they had used, and how.
Who must have gone first. Him last. But more than that I am
afraid I knew exactly how they felt, as the moment came on

them over dinner, and they rushed—in some terrible parody of joy—into each others' arms.

I locked the door behind me, and wondered how long I could keep this to myself.

THERE IS A sound that comes at dawn. I have never heard it. I wake in a room full of echoes, holding my breath, and lie beside Ell sleeping, and watch the light change in the room. I cannot escape the sense that I have missed something important. But as the light grows, the room around me is utterly ordinary.

I rise from the bed, the cold floor at my feet telling me again I am awake, the world is real. Through a silence fragile as old age I inspect each room, and everything is as we left it. But in each room, the objects I find—the chair with the book face-down upon its arm, my binoculars on the windowsill—seem to be holding a pose, waiting for my back to turn. Only the kitchen clock confesses, filling the room with the catch and release of its cogs. In a distant, unconscious way I hear the sound of water flowing in the gorge, whispering dimly. The falls are almost frozen over.

I wring back the curtains, snap up the shades, flush the rooms with light and nothing moves. In the kitchen I heat the kettle to a scream, bang pots, and overcook the oats. Upstairs, Ell is moving slowly; she showers, the pipes shudder and groan, the wind picks up outside. In the feeders, finches hiss and flutter, fighting for a perch. A dog lopes hip-deep through the yard, barking bright blue clouds of breath at the treetops, where four crows cling to the waving limbs. They flap and caw, caw a senseless monody. Over all of us, gray clouds pour ceaselessly into the east.

The wind has blown for days. I wonder how much longer it can blow before the country west of us lies in a vacuum, and dogs and crows, finches and clouds freeze solid, and the trees' metallic branches thrill faintly against the stars. I have dreamed this. I have been dreaming of the stars as they once were, as I will never see them again, unless there is after all another life after this one, in a cold and airless west.

I woke again this morning among the booming echoes. Through the window I saw the morning star, failing, dim in the sick gleam that made my hand a skeleton on the curtain. Between my ribs my heart was thunderous in its hollow, ticking off the seconds of the dawn.

A RESTLESSNESS TOOK me out of the house today, on a final, senseless errand. I took the car downtown to fill its tank, though I have nowhere left to go, no errands left unrun.

As I coasted down the long hill into town, I noticed that the odometer was less than ten miles from turning over. This fact—this string of nines rolling up under the quivering needle—loomed before me much larger than I wanted it to. The windshield hazed, and the large, familiar hands that held the wheel seemed not my own. They are older than I noticed them last—the skin is drier, nicked with scars I don't remember, and a gold band glints at one finger.

As I came down the block I saw a banner over the pumps.

FREE GAS

it read, in hand-drawn black. The sign sighed and billowed in the breeze, but nothing else moved: the pumps were deserted, the street beyond stretching silent and empty down to the frozen lake.

By the time I stopped the car, I was almost laughing, glad to have my mood broken by this sorry joke. I have given over too often to self-pity: it is only a car. Through the glass, still decked with offers of anti-freeze, I saw the owner dimly, seated at his desk, and thought I saw him smiling.

Gasoline spilled from the neck of the tank. The trigger gave a dull clunk and went limp.

The door to the cashier's office was locked. The knob rattled loudly in my hand, but the figure smiling by the open cash drawer did not move. I stooped to peer through the glass. He sat upright, his mouth and eyes wide open.

I took a winding route back home, through the empty streets. Not everyone is dead: as the sun set, windows lit in many houses. The people at the power station are still at their posts. I drove past every drugstore I could think of, and every one was empty, dark. On some of them, the doors stood open; others had their windows smashed. The street by a liquor store glittered and flashed. I drove home wondering, What are they waiting for?

I could not think of an answer.

At the sound of my key in the lock, Ell pulled open the door, rushed at me, and grabbed my shoulders. As I thought horribly of what could be wrong she was saying, —Where have you been? and, —I was sure, and, —Where were you?

I couldn't speak. We did not fight. Normally, in such a case, we would, and eventually would have understood. I couldn't. There was something on my tongue, even now I cannot say what, only that a fear of speaking welled up and stifled me. When she ran weeping from the room, guilt stabbed me, but I could not explain. I walked upstairs and closed the study door, sat here at my desk for a long time before turning on the lights.

THE MORNING IS bright. Outside the house the icicles are running, and water echoes loudly in the drains. Fresh air stirs the curtains, breathing in at the window opened for the first time in months. The January thaw has come, but a few days past the turning of the year, rushing as if to make the time. The air is piercing, fresh and sweet. It buoys me with an indiscriminate urge to do something—nothing I can name. It speaks tongueless, as varying and insistent as the water in the drains. The fresh air blows past my ears, whispering promises of spring.

When I came down from my study late last night, Ell was reading in her accustomed chair, her feet tucked underneath her legs against the cold. She looked up, angry and compact. I knew she would not speak—that it was up to me. But what was there to say? A minute passed, drawn out into a wire that tightened between us. I wanted to flinch—to run away. But where was there to run?

From where I stood in the doorway, her face seemed a shield held out against me. But in the curve of her lower lip, I saw a trace of motion, a sustained, suppressed tremor. It told me something of what she must have felt when I did not come home—and what she must be feeling now. I understood the offering of her face then, the cost it exacted as the minutes wore on and the muscles of her neck grew tired, quivering. I met her eyes, and the intensity of the look that met me seized me out of vagueness into something solid, here and real.

At that moment the lights flickered, and my heart leapt with an animal despair— dumb, and damned so. The lights went yellow, faded slowly to orange, red, and as the darkness closed in around us, I saw in her face—motionless still, and pale—the same mute despair, and then it was dark.

We found candles in the kitchen. By their light we made love upstairs, in a bed piled high with blankets. The clock beside us was stopped at a quarter to, and the candles held at bay the sky's sick light. We were awkward; we were shy. I could not remember the last time we had broken the unspoken agreement that for months has kept us from each other.

A SILENCE THIS morning disturbed me as I stood, awash in the morning light, at the kitchen sink. Something was missing. I listened, until I realized that what I missed was the sound of birds at the feeders: the crack and scatter of the seeds, the whirr of wings—the ungainly thud of the jays. I wiped steam from the windows. Every feeder hung deserted, full of seed, shuddering gently in the wind. I watch, and no birds come. Hours have passed, and I have not seen or heard them yet.

Perhaps they know. Perhaps some message came to them. I

hope so. I hope that, even now, someone in a southern kitchen is wondering at the chickadees, the juncos, the titmice, and the nuthatch, upside down, inspecting some unnaturally sweet and tender fruit.

THERE HAD BEEN another wreck. Both of us stayed seated long after the booming died away. The falls have frozen over at last; no sound rose to fill the silence. We sat throughout the afternoon, as the light faded and the sun went down for what must have been the last time—a dull, dim-red extinction. It disappeared and left behind a sky as blank as if the constellations had been destroyed. Perhaps they have. The moon rose soon after, waning, gibbous, sick in a sea of spoiled milk, and still we sat.

Ell rose, groaning a little with the effort it takes her now to stand. She shuffled out to the kitchen. I heard her fumbling in the drawer where the candles are, rattling hollow objects for a time that stretched out far too long. I couldn't bear it. When she returned, her face alight, I stood abruptly, unable to look at her.

I think she knew, as I walked out the door, that I was not going to the gorge.

The streets lay deep in snow, and as I drove down the steep and winding road that ends in the bridge across the gorge, I lost control, fishtailed out onto the span sideways for the rail. Someone laughed as I spun, the railing moving wrongway by the windshield; then I was stopped, turned sideways in the middle of the bridge.

I got out of the car, stepping out onto the steel grid. Wind whistled up at me. I looked down through the deck; a dozen dark shapes lay at the ends of scars scraped in the show. I walked to the western rail and looked out over the valley where the gorge opens and falls finally into the lake. On the far hill shone a constellation of kerosene and candles, flickering dimly across the miles. Down in the town, a brighter glow grew into a blaze of buildings burning at the center. On the north wind came no sound, no smell of smoke, only the wind.

In the southwest, a dim glow, as the sunset faded into the ashen light of the sky. No evening star.

Then I was driving, fast again, swerving around curves I had never seen before, headlights doused. I remember nothing until three deer stood and faced me in the road.

Then there was light, shining in my eyes. They lifted me by the shoulders, headfirst through the window of my car although I clutched the wheel and cried. I saw a tire turning, spinning slowly in the air.

Then there was light again, and warmth, a chair, and hands rubbing mine and feeling up and down my arms and legs, voices asking, —Hurt? Talk?—a voice whispering, —Shock.

They put my fingers around a cup, where heat thawed feeling out of numb nothing. Something hot trickled down my throat.

And the first thing I saw was a tree, standing in the corner, shedding its needles on the floor. I thought: I missed Christmas, and: It was all a dream. The room solidified: a kitchen, plank floor, wood stove, iron washstand, water heater in the far corner. Warm light and the smell of kerosene. A man in coveralls, about my age, but the lines in his face had cut more deeply, the hand with which he slid the teacup back across the table was a farmer's hand, old already. As I reached out to take the cup, he watched me critically.

—You're not the first, he said.

I nodded, unable to explain.

He nodded back, indicating my hand. —You're married.

I nodded again.

—Alive?

Again.

The man paused, looked away from me, and cleared his throat. —Do you want to go back?

I feel tears on my face. My voice makes no sound; the room seems to expand around me, leaving me in darkness. It is too late for words.

I heard a chair move, and felt a hand on my shoulder. —I'll go warm up the truck.

The man did not return. I heard an engine catch, roar, and settle into a rapid idle. A woman, in a faded print, and herself worn thin enough to show the pulse at her temple, a tremor in her jaw, each bone and tendon of her hand, sat around the corner of the table. She reached out to touch the tabletop before me, paused.

—Your wife alone? Her voice was hoarse.

I wondered what she might mean, and looked around the room. Through an open door I saw three children all alike in dingy pastel pajamas, staring back at me.

—We let them stay up late tonight, she apologized. —When

we talk about it, they don't understand. But they like to stay up. We wanted to do something for them. She looked at them, and whispered, —Do you know what I mean?

I stood abruptly, caught myself with a hand on her shoulder and staggered into her lap. Embarrassed, she gave me her thin arm, and, biting her lower lip, led me to the truck. There she whispered to her husband, and, with a shy glance at me, kissed him long and urgently. Then we were gone.

The road was drifted deep where snow had blown across the fields. The clouds had broken before the rising wind. The moon burned bright at our backs, the only thing in the ghostly sky. It shone unnaturally bright. I felt it pushing, as it brightened by the minute, behind us.

The man drove fast, his need for haste twice mine. Deer were everywhere. They stood in silent groups of twos and threes beside the road. Smaller shapes, writhing in the headlights, fled before us. Overhead, darkness dotted the sky, flitting from horizon to horizon as if the graves gave up their dead. The face of the man beside me was taut in the dim green light of the speedometer. He swerved to miss something that froze before us—a skunk—and silently drove on.

He turned on the radio, tuned from static to a voice beseeching to the sound of running water, then fire, then large masses breaking, waves upon a shore, marching feet, applause, a voice explaining, violins, a chorus shouting, a man singing

Froh, wie seine Sonnen fliegen
Durch des Himmels prächt'gen Plan.

He switched it off. —Last night there was hymns, down from Canada. You could tell it was hymns, even in French.

One road to the city was blocked by fire: black against the flames, men and women were dancing, singing, in tuxedos and gowns, diamonds flaming like stars.

The bridge from the north was destroyed.

The way from the south was blocked by a creature I cannot describe.

The door was unlocked. It opened into the dark hall, and I stepped in. I stood in the doorway, seeing no reason to shut the door behind me. The house was as cold as a crypt, and—I knew without having to ask—as empty. I wondered where she would be when the time caught her. I hoped the time would find her ready. I would never be, and saw no reason to wait, not any longer.

I went to the kitchen and pulled the stool up to the sink, and fumbling open the casing of the clock I found the vial I had hidden the night we fought. Not all of the drugstores had been closed that evening. I am more coward than I seem. I stood on the stool, the vial warming in my palm, and tried to remember something I had forgotten. The silence in the room was complete.

The clock at my ear was silent.

She reached up and took the vial away. —I poured it out. It's just food coloring now.

How foolish I was to think anything would remain hidden! She helped me from the stool, stopping me as I started to fall. Her hair was cold, smelling of the outdoors. For a long time we were silent. For the space of half an hour, nothing mattered.

Then she moved, reached up a hand to touch my face. The light of the moon had brightened abruptly, as if a window shade had snapped up. As the light and silence grew, I felt the spell that has kept me speechless breaking. But when I bent to her ear and started to whisper, she placed her hand gently over my mouth and held it. I understood: there is nothing to say.

We stood together in the growing light, the thunder rumbling in the distance, drawing nearer, and I shrugged away impulses that no longer had meaning—to speech, to fear, to sorrow. I felt laughter growing inside me. Certainly she was laughing. At the window, moonlight poured in.

Ellen spoke. —Is there anything you want?

—Yes. The words came easily. —I want to finish something.

And at the door of this room, she left me. —I'll call if I need you.

LITTLE REMAINS. She is calling. The moon burns still brighter with each passing second, leaves my hand too slow to record, to report. I must end now.

But before the end we will speak once more, of everything that matters: of the brightness of the moon; of the birds still flying dark against the sky; of the man who brought me here; of the hours that she waited; of what we would name the child; of the grace of everything that dies; of the love that moves the sun and other stars.

Terrence Holt began writing the stories in this collection while he was earning MFA and PhD degrees in English from Cornell University. His first published story, "Charybdis," appeared originally in the *Kenyon Review* and was included in the O. *Henry Prize Stories 1980*. After a decade teaching English literature and creative writing, Holt enrolled in night school premedical courses at the University of Pennsylvania and went on to earn his MD from the University of North Carolina at Chapel Hill, where he now holds academic and clinical appointments in the Department of Social Medicine and the Division of Geriatric Medicine. "I went into medicine for reasons having nothing to do with writing," he says. "It was only after I'd been at it for several years that I realized I'd found another way of doing the same thing."

"In both," Holt explains, "I'm intimately involved with the limits of human existence—of life, of compassion, of our capacity to understand ourselves in our world. For me, these stories are more than anything else about where stories come from, and where they take us. They're about the moment-by-moment process by which our brains convince us that the world exists, and the gaps in that process as well. Those flaws in the illusion are what I want to capture. They're the chinks in the structure where mystery gets in and haunts our lives— and through which one day we slip into eternity."

In addition to his writing and the practice of medicine, Holt is an avid amateur astronomer and has written a handbook for amateurs, *The Universe Next Door*. He lives in Chapel Hill with his wife and two sons, with whom he haunts the flea markets and bass ponds of the Piedmont, respectively. He also plays the Highland bagpipes—very badly, he says, but very, very loudly.